Take Me Again

CARLY PHILLIPS

All alpha all the time, Sebastian Knight's confidence never wavers. At least not until Ashley Easton walks back into his life, wanting nothing to do with the playboy who broke her heart.

Sebastian Knight is a closer. Be it a business deal or the woman of his choice, everything he wants is his for the taking. Sexy and irresistible, a wink, a smile, or a handshake always seals the deal. Until Ashley returns at the worst possible time, and everything unravels around him.

The Ashley who returns is sassy and sexy—everything Sebastian craves and he wants a second chance. Despite her reluctance, his sex appeal makes it harder and harder to keep him at arm's length.

Sebastian might have a talent for sealing the deal, but Ashley is no longer easily charmed. This time he's going to have to work to win.

Chapter One

S EBASTIAN KNIGHT'S HEAD pounded like a motherfucker, and light streamed in from the window, piercing through one eye and into his brain. He groaned and rolled over, burying his face in the pillow. At twenty-six, wasn't he too damned old for a hangover like this? Yeah, he'd have to remember that the next time he picked up a glass of tequila and asked the bartender to keep them coming to celebrate closing a huge deal with his brothers for their tech company, Knight Time Technology. Except Ethan and Parker had gone home after toasting their success. After that, Sebastian didn't remember much.

A flash of red flickered through his mind. A woman with flame-hued hair had joined him at the bar. He recalled the unusual color and the obviously fake but very tempting breasts that protruded over the top of her tight dress, along with his body's reaction to her assets.

Shit.

Was he alone now?

He lifted his head and opened his eyes, not seeing anyone lying beside him and not recognizing where he was, but from the abundance of white furniture and the generic feel and look of the place, it was definitely a hotel room. An upscale suite but a hotel nevertheless.

Memory came back in small increments.

The deal they'd landed was to supply state-of-the-art locks to a defense contractor. They'd outbid some major players when Sebastian had stepped in and closed the deal, something he excelled at and his brothers counted on him to do.

They'd headed to The Bar at the Baccarat Hotel in order to celebrate. Toasted their success. He'd taken his first sip of Don Julio 1942, and it had gone down smooth.

And though he might not remember making the elevator ride up to this hotel room, he was here. Which meant *he'd* be the one making his escape from this one-night stand, hopefully without too much of a scene.

The click of a door sounded, and the redhead walked out of the bathroom, a towel wrapped around her body. Her cleavage was as ample as he remembered, her hair as red, her face? Not as pretty as he'd have hoped or as she'd probably appeared to his drunk self.

He scrubbed a hand over his gritty eyes and pushed up to a sitting position.

"Morning, lover." She started toward him, her stride confident, but he wasn't in the mood for small talk or sex.

Instead of waiting for her to ease onto the mattress alongside him, he slid out of bed and rose to his feet. He glanced down to find his pants, grateful to see a torn condom package on the floor beside his clothes. Thank God, even in his inebriated state, he'd been smart about wrapping up.

"Aren't you going to stick around for a morning quickie?" she asked as she opened the towel, revealing her naked body, his for the taking.

His dick didn't even perk up at the sight of her tits, and he shook his head. "Sorry, doll," he said, because he didn't remember her name, dressing as he spoke. "I have a meeting I need to get to."

Her pout was real. "Didn't you have a good time last night?" she asked, sounding hurt, fumbling to cover herself with the towel again in the face of his rejection.

I don't remember wasn't what she wanted to hear.

He zipped his trousers and slid on his white dress shirt, buttoning up. "It was great. But now it's over," he said, knowing he had to be very clear about his intentions or lack thereof. Socks and shoes went on next, and he was dressed and ready to go.

He patted his pockets, double-checking for his wallet and cell phone, and headed for the door. As awkward as this was, no need to prolong it or make it worse.

"Bastard," she muttered.

And after he'd pulled the door closed, he heard what sounded like a shoe being thrown as the door clicked shut behind him. Yeah, he really was getting too old for this shit.

He pulled out his phone, only to discover he'd turned off the ringer sometime during the night and his brothers had tried to reach him numerous times. So had his younger sister, Sierra.

He narrowed his gaze. Why the hell had everyone been looking for him?

He took the elevator down to the first floor and walked through the lobby, across the white marble, and out into the Manhattan sunshine before hitting redial and calling his oldest brother, Ethan. When the call went directly to voicemail, he dialed Parker next.

"Where the fuck have you been?" his middle sibling all but yelled.

"Calm yourself, Switzerland," he said, using the nickname the family had for Parker that had begun during his championship skiing days and stuck because he refused to take sides in family arguments, always tending to remain neutral. "I'm here now. What's going on?"

Squinting into the sun, Sebastian hailed the first empty cab he saw, the driver coming to a skidding stop on his side of the street.

"Mandy died, Sebastian."

He froze, his hand on the taxi door handle. "Say that again."

"Mandy died," he said of Ethan's wife. "I've been with E all night. So has Sierra. So get your ass to his place, like, yesterday."

The cab driver honked the horn, letting Sebastian know he'd better climb in the back seat or the man would take off. He opened the door and slid onto the taped-up pleather, his heart heavy and thudding inside his chest.

"What happened?" he asked through his thick throat and dry mouth.

Everyone loved Ethan's wife, Amanda, Mandy for short, who had been an executive at Knight Time Technology.

"Buddy, where to?" the cab driver asked impatiently.

He gave the address of the apartment building uptown that the company owned, where all the siblings resided.

Parker waited for Sebastian to finish before he answered. "Accidental overdose."

"What the fuck?" Mandy didn't take drugs, not that he knew of.

"It's a long story." Parker sounded exhausted. "Just come home and I'll explain everything."

"How's Ethan?" he asked, worried about his older brother, who felt it was his job to look after everyone else.

He'd taken on the role of caretaker after their mother passed away when Sebastian had been fifteen. Only nineteen at the time, Ethan had stepped up because, frankly, their father had never been the responsible parent.

"About as good as you'd expect," Parker muttered.

Which meant not good at all.

He needed to get to his sibling, but the Manhattan traffic moved at a snail's pace and the ride seemed to take forever. He closed his eyes throughout the trip uptown and pictured Ethan's wife, a petite brunette with a vibrant personality. Granted, she'd been more subdued lately, her shoulder surgery almost two years ago having been hard on her physically and mentally. But an accidental overdose? It didn't compute.

The cab finally came to a stop. He shoved his credit card into the slot and completed the transaction, climbed out of the car, and made his way past the doorman, into the building and up the elevator, another ride that seemed endless.

Arriving at Ethan's door, he knocked once and Sierra let him in, wrapping her arms around him, her smaller body shaking as she cried. The Knight siblings were each two years apart and he was close to his twenty-four-year-old baby sister. He walked into the apartment, Sierra holding on to him, and found his brothers in the living room.

She stepped away, sniffing as she sank into an oversized chair. From his place on the sofa, Ethan rose to his feet. His brother's dark hair was disheveled, his eyes bloodshot and red.

In silence, Sebastian stepped forward and pulled him into a brotherly embrace. "I'm sorry, man," he said at last. "What happened?"

Ethan straightened to his full height. "I came home. Thought she was napping but I couldn't wake her up. I called 911 but it was too late." His voice sounded like gravel, the pain etched in his face raw and real.

"Parker–" Sebastian gestured to his brother, who was now sitting on the far side of the couch. "Parker said it was an overdose, but I don't understand. Overdose on what?"

"Sit," Ethan said and Sebastian chose a matching chair next to Sierra's. "It was Oxy."

"What?" He couldn't believe what he was hearing.

Ethan shook his head, obviously at a loss.

"It started after the shoulder surgery," Parker said, taking over when Ethan's voice failed him. "The doctors loaded her up with drugs to help with the pain. We had no idea they kept giving them to her until she was hooked."

Sebastian blinked in surprise, whether at Mandy's addiction he'd known nothing about or his middle brother's use of the word *we* when describing the situation, he couldn't be sure. The one thing Sebastian did know, he wasn't part of that *we*.

"Shit. I'm sorry." He ran a hand through his already disheveled hair.

As he began to put the pieces together of the story his brother was telling him, Sebastian reeled with what, so far, had gone unsaid. "You aren't shocked by this, and not because Ethan told you last night, after Mandy died." From the matter-of-fact way Parker had relayed the information, as if he'd already digested it and it had settled inside him, it was obvious. "You've known all along."

Parker merely nodded.

He glanced at his sister, who sat wide-eyed on the chair next to his. "What about you? Did you know?" he asked.

She swallowed hard. "Mandy told me recently that she was having problems. I talked to Ethan about it," she admitted.

"So everyone knew something. But me." Sebastian rose to his feet, hurt and betrayal warring with anger, combining with grief inside him.

Parker met his gaze. "I was there the first time he found her pills. That's all."

But Sebastian sensed there was more to it. That he'd been left out of the loop for a reason. He glanced at Ethan.

"We didn't want to bother you with serious shit," Ethan said. "You didn't *need* to know. We were handling it."

"I didn't need to know or you didn't trust me to keep it to myself?" Sebastian asked, the truth crystallizing without his brother having to say anything. "Admit it. You were afraid I'd share info, like the Williamson deal."

It'd been his first year in the family business, one started by their great-great-grandfather, who'd been a locksmith. Legend had it he'd been such an expert on locks, he'd broken Billy the Kid out of jail. These days, the company supplied high-tech security for smart buildings and state-of-the-art corporate parks, competed for contracts with the most lucrative companies in the world, and owned enough patents to keep them exceedingly wealthy.

At the height of bidding on a particular project,

Sebastian had been having a drink with a beautiful blonde. He hadn't known at the time she was the daughter of the man against whom they were bidding for a contract.

He'd been young, cocky, and stupid. She'd been busty, which distracted him, and extremely bright. He'd bragged they were sure to win, that nobody would come close to their number. She'd hung on him, praised him, made him feel important, and he'd admitted that they'd maxed out their bid. They couldn't go lower on their proposal. It was all the information she'd needed to grab the contract out from under them. Because of his big mouth.

Ethan blew out a harsh breath. "Fine, I didn't want it getting out that Mandy had a problem, okay? I figured the fewer people who knew, the better."

He straightened his shoulders and glared at his sibling. "You can't let it go? You were handling it as a family and didn't think I needed to be part of it? I couldn't have helped? I couldn't have been there for you?" he asked, voice rising.

"Not with something this sensitive!" Ethan shot back.

Parker rose, stepped over to Sebastian, and placed a hand on his shoulder. "Now's not the time," he told him, putting himself in between his brothers.

Glancing at Ethan, shoulders hunched, his pain

obvious, Sebastian agreed. "He's right. You're hurting and you don't need to deal with this shit right now."

There'd be time for Sebastian's anger at his family later, after they'd all grieved for Mandy.

ASHLEY EASTON SAT across the table from her boyfriend of six months at the Ivy West Street London, a fixture on London's social and dining scene for decades. She was surprised Jonathan had chosen such an upscale, see-and-be-seen restaurant for their Saturday night date. Usually they went to more casual places.

Redesigned in 2015, the decor boasted a shimmering central dining bar, harlequin stained-glass windows, and oak paneling. She'd dressed up for the occasion, a little black dress and heels, as had he, dressed as he was in a three-piece navy suit and red tie.

They'd met working at the same accounting firm, and Jonathan Davies was, at heart, a kind man. With his dark brown hair trimmed just so, courtesy of the barber he saw weekly, brown eyes, and a serious personality, he was the epitome of what would be a Wall Street guy at home in the States. But Ashley had been living in London, thanks to a job offer straight out of university. After being sent to boarding school abroad at the age of sixteen, she'd never gone back home.

New York City hadn't been her home anyway.

The waiter had removed their dinner plates and cleaned off the crumbs on the table. He returned with strawberries and cream, placing the dishes down.

"Oh! We didn't order—"

"I thought I'd surprise you. I know how much you enjoy fresh fruit," Jonathan said. "Would you like some more champagne?"

She smiled. "Yes, please."

As if he'd been listening, the waiter arrived at her elbow. He picked up the bottle from the ice bucket and filled both of their glasses.

"Thank you," she murmured.

Jonathan leaned forward, his gaze on hers as he reached across the table and clasped her hand. "You look so lovely tonight."

She smiled at the compliment. It was unlike him to be demonstrative in any way, no public displays of affection. British stiff upper lip and all that. "Thank you. You're looking mighty dapper yourself. I have to admit I was surprised you picked such an upscale place for dinner."

"I had a reason," he said, red suddenly highlighting his cheekbones.

Jonathan didn't blush, but it was an indication of how off he'd been tonight. Antsy throughout dinner.

Checking his watch. Asking her if she was finished with her meal not long after it had been served.

She glanced at their intertwined hands. "Jonathan, do you have something on your mind?"

He shifted in his seat. Cleared his throat. "Yes. As a matter of fact, I do."

She tilted her head, waiting for him to explain.

"Ashley, you'd say we get on quite nicely, yes?"

She nodded. "Of course we do." They enjoyed the same restaurants, her friends liked him, and they rarely ran out of things to talk about. This one conversation excluded, it was a comfortable relationship, a safe one, but not one with sexual sparks. Still, it worked for her, having learned at a very young age what desire and acting on your baser instincts wrought.

Her parents had loved one another but her blue-collar dad, a man she recalled only by his warm, booming voice, died when she was four. And her mother had given up on love, focusing on financial security instead. She'd gone from wealthy man to wealthy man, and had even agreed to have Ashley sent away. Or maybe it'd been her idea in the first place. As a result, like her mother, Ashley no longer believed in love, happily ever after, or even marriage. Unlike her mother, she wanted to rely on herself.

Because everyone who was supposed to look out for her had abandoned her. From what she'd seen, what was the point in giving her heart? That's why this relationship worked for her. She and Jonathan were compatible, no explosive chemistry to mess up her head and make her believe in things that weren't possible.

She glanced at the man across the table. "You can talk to me," she said. "What's wrong?"

He shook his head. "I'm hoping everything is right." He released her hand and lowered his arm, clearly pulling something out of his pants pocket and coming up with a small black velvet box.

Her stomach turned over. "Oh my God."

"Will you marry me, Ashley?" He opened the box and she stared at the solitaire ring in total and utter shock.

She hadn't expected a proposal. Not so early in their relationship and really not at all. She'd never given him any indication that the relationship was headed in that direction or that she wanted something permanent. She enjoyed Jonathan and her time with him ... but marriage? She shook her head. That wasn't something she wanted or desired.

"I–"

"Think about it," he said, interrupting her. "We make a good couple and I've fallen in love with you," he said, his voice warming.

She bit down on the inside of her cheek, wishing

he'd told her *that* before proposing. She would have slowed things down immediately.

"Oh, Jonathan. I'm not ... ready to get married," she said, hoping she was letting him down gently.

Another version of *it's not you, it's me.* But she was being honest. To her, marriage meant love and commitment and the happily ever after she didn't think was possible for herself.

His sparkling eyes dulled as she turned him down.

"I'm sorry," she said. "I didn't realize you felt... I just..." She trailed off, unsure of what else to say. She'd hurt him and that was the last thing she'd wanted to do.

"I hope you'll consider it," he said, persistent to the end. "You don't have to say anything now." He closed the box and tucked the ring back into his pants pocket. "But I'll be holding on to this. And hoping."

She shook her head. "Please don't." Her heart squeezed as she spoke, because he was a kind man and would make some woman a good husband. Just not her. "I like you, a lot, and I enjoy your company." She forced herself to meet his gaze despite the painful churning in her stomach. "But I don't love you. And I don't see my feelings growing that way. In fact, I don't believe in falling in love."

She kept her voice gentle as she broke it off with him. "Given all that..." She pointed to the ring. "I think we should end things." She spoke as gently as she could.

"I'm not going to give up on hope," he said, surprising her. She hadn't seen him as the overly persistent type, but here he was, not wanting to let her go. "People have built solid marriages on less."

Yet between the two of them, neither had communicated enough feelings to get to this point. She couldn't believe he'd put them in this position. And though she'd miss him and the time they spent together, she just didn't love him.

Did she trust any man enough to fall in love? A question for another time.

She sighed just as her phone rang from inside her purse. She didn't want to take the call, didn't want to make him feel less valued than he already did.

"Check it." He gestured with a tip of his head toward where her handbag hung on the chair. "It might be important."

She nodded, assuming he needed time after his rejected proposal, and pulled her phone from her bag. She glanced down to see Ethan Knight's name flashing on the screen.

Ethan was the closest thing she had to a brother. In fact, he had been her brother once, in the short time her mother had been married to his father. A few years, only six months of which she'd lived under the same roof with him and his two brothers and sister. But he'd stepped up for her, and as a result, her relationship with him was important to her.

She glanced at Jonathan. "One minute?" she asked and he nodded.

She answered the phone. "Hi, Ethan. Everything okay?" He didn't usually call during his business hours in the United States.

"It's Parker." Ethan's middle brother, who she hadn't had any contact with since her mother and his father had sent her away to boarding school. He'd been the quietest one, busy with his skiing and training for the Olympics.

"Is everything okay?" she immediately asked.

"I'm going through the numbers in Ethan's phone and I know he'd want me to call you."

"What's wrong?" She stiffened with panic. "Is Ethan okay?"

"It's Mandy," Parker said. "She ... passed away last night."

Dizziness assaulted her. Ethan's wife. The woman he loved, as much as she'd let him, anyway. "Oh my God."

"Ashley?" Jonathan placed his napkin on the table, and leaned forward.

She held up a hand. "What happened?" she asked Parker.

"Accidental overdose."

She swallowed hard. "How is he?"

"Shaken up. Hurting. I know he kept in touch with you over the years and you two are close. He'd want you to know."

"Thank you for calling. How … how is the family?" she forced herself to ask.

"It's been a shock but we're dealing," Parker said. "I saw your email was in E's contacts. I'll send you the funeral information."

"Thank you," she said again. "Goodbye."

"Bye."

She disconnected the call, eyes glazed with unshed tears for Ethan and Mandy, a woman she'd liked very much.

She brushed at the tears in her eyes, worried about Ethan. He wasn't used to relying on other people. Instead he was the caretaker, she thought. Knowing him, he would try to push forward, but he was the brother who had stepped into the parental role his real father didn't know how to perform. And now he'd need someone to handle things once the immediate shock wore off and reality settled in.

He had his siblings—Parker, who was obviously taking charge, and Sebastian, who, as far as she knew, was still the playboy he'd always been. He also had his younger sister, Sierra. But they'd all be hurting. Ashley could lift the burden and be there for Ethan much as he'd always been there for her over the years.

Jonathan cleared his throat, bringing her back to the present. "What's going on?" he asked. "You look upset."

She met his gaze. "That was Parker, Ethan Knight's brother."

Although Jonathan knew she and Ethan Knight were close friends, he didn't know her past with the family and how she'd ended up on this side of the pond, as he liked to say.

And didn't that explain just another reason why she couldn't marry him, she thought. He didn't know the most intimate details of her life—because she hadn't chosen to share them with him.

"His wife passed away," she explained. "And I need to go back."

"I'm sorry to hear that, but back? To New York?" he asked, sounding surprised.

She nodded. "Ethan is like a brother and he'll need me now."

"But for how long?" Jonathan asked, his expression puzzled, as if he was trying to figure out where he fit into her plans.

"I don't know." But considering she'd just declined his proposal, distance would be a good thing, she thought, though she wouldn't say such a thing aloud.

She didn't need the stress of him pressuring her or her friends asking her how she could have turned him down.

Jonathan paid the check in awkward silence and he drove her home, their parting even more uncomfortable. In her mind, they were over. She cared about him and was sad, but their relationship had been more about convenience than love. And right now she could only focus on Ethan. The one true friend she'd ever had at a time when she otherwise would have been completely lost.

And that meant she was headed back to the States. She couldn't call it home. Sebastian had made sure of that. If only returning home didn't mean dealing with the only man who'd ever held her heart.

Before she'd locked it up for good.

Chapter Two

THE DAY OF the funeral, Sebastian tried to act as a buffer for his brother, but people had come to pay their respects, and they wanted to talk to Ethan in person. The family gathered, Ethan, Sebastian, Parker, and Sierra, in a small room where a revolving door of guests came in and went out again. Sebastian lost track of who he'd seen, personal friends and professional colleagues giving their condolences, but there was a book outside that would keep track of who'd come and gone.

His best buddy, Ryder Hammond, was there, a long-time friend of the family and Sierra's one-time boyfriend. Back in high school, they'd gotten together, and man, it'd been serious fast, only to burn out when Ryder panicked and broke up with her before her graduation. These days, Sierra was engaged to a great guy, who was away on business and couldn't make it back for the funeral. Even so, they all approved of the man for Sierra, and as far as Sebastian knew, she'd made her peace with Ryder. But that didn't mean he didn't catch lingering looks between them at family gatherings that made him uneasy and left him wondering if they had unfinished business.

In fact, even now, as Ryder stood by the window in the small room, talking to Parker, his gaze drifted to Sierra. Sebastian glanced at his friend, eyebrow cocked until Ryder looked his way. Caught, he smirked and turned away.

Sebastian shook his head and glanced at his oblivious sister, who was talking to one of their father's old friends.

Alexander had offered to cancel a planned cruise to the Mediterranean with wife number four, but Ethan had insisted he keep his plans. Nobody wanted the drama that came with Candy, the guilt and heavy sighs that would inevitably occur because she'd had to skip the trip she'd been dying to go on. And in truth, the man had sounded relieved.

Sebastian's mouth was dry and he needed water. The pitcher next to Ethan was empty, and he picked up the silver holder and took it outside.

Sierra joined him, catching up with him by the water cooler near the front office. "I needed some air, too," she said, fanning herself. Her cheeks were flushed, her brown hair with blonde highlights falling out of a bun and across her cheek.

"Anything wrong?" he asked. "Besides the obvious?" He gestured to their depressing surroundings, really wondering if the blush in her face had anything to do with Ryder's lingering looks, but he didn't want to mention the man and risk upsetting her.

She shook her head. "Funerals just aren't easy, and I feel so bad for Ethan."

He pulled her into a hug and kissed the top of her head. "Are you okay?"

She glanced up at him and nodded. "Best I can be."

"I get that." He filled the water pitcher, condensation dripping to the floor. "Ready to get back?"

Drawing in a deep breath, she nodded. "Let's go."

Together, they walked back into the sitting room and excused themselves, easing past a new crowd of people, making their way to where Ethan sat. As he reached his brother, Sebastian drew up short. A blonde woman stood beside Ethan, hand on his shoulder, head bent close to his as she whispered in his ear.

There was a closeness to their contact, and the longer Sebastian stared, the more he sensed something familiar about the female comforting his brother. Familiar but he couldn't place her. Until she lifted her head and her gaze locked with his, sky-blue eyes opening wide in recognition.

Jesus fuck. What was *she* doing here?

He swallowed hard, his gaze skimming over her, taking her in. Her face had slimmed down over the years, her cheekbones more sculpted. Her beautiful features were still put together, so striking she took his breath away. And her lips were just as full and kissable – and he ought to know, finding it all too easy to conjure the taste of her in his mouth. When it came to her, his memory was crystal clear.

"It's Ashley," his sister said from beside him. "Oh my God, we haven't seen her in years."

"No, we haven't."

He curled his hands into tight fists, the sight of her stirring up recollections he'd never quite forgotten but wasn't thrilled to have resurrected. What he'd done, what he hadn't done... One of his not-so-finest moments. He couldn't say he hadn't thought about her over the years, he had, but the thoughts came with regrets.

His father had married her mother when he'd been eighteen, Ashley sixteen, and the attraction between her and Sebastian had been instantaneous. But even at his wildest, he'd known she was too young. Too vulnerable for him to desire with the depth of feeling that he had.

As he watched her with Ethan now, Sebastian realized she hadn't just shown up out of nowhere. She and his brother were obviously close, which left him reeling with the knowledge of yet another secret kept from him.

At the sight of her, his mind went back to the past. She'd moved into his house along with her mother, another one of the women his father chose who wanted his money. Ashley had been adrift, alone. Often sad and lonely.

He'd taken to sitting up at night, talking to her. They'd gotten along, had a lot in common, both of them lacking real parental figures. But he hadn't missed how she'd looked at him any more than he could have denied how his body had responded to her curves, the breasts beneath her tee shirts, braless, nipples poking through, and the sweet shape of her ass in her sweats.

His hands had itched to touch as much as his lips wanted to kiss. He'd hadn't had much self-control in those days, and looking back, he'd been a powder keg—and it had only been a matter of time.

Six months into her living in the house, he'd gone out to a party and gotten drunk, coming home to find Ashley waiting up for him. She'd clearly been drinking herself, informing him she'd taken vodka from his father's stash, refilling the bottle with water. Clever girl even then. When she'd walked up to him, pressed her supple body against him, kissing him with young abandon, he'd lost all good intentions.

She'd rubbed her breasts against his chest and licked at his lips with her tongue ... and his arms had come around her, yanking her into him. His mouth had plundered hers and they made out like wild teenagers right there in the hall outside his father's study. His tongue deep in her mouth, soft yearning sounds coming from her throat.

Yeah, it'd been two a.m. and they should have been safe. But his father had come downstairs to the kitchen at the moment Sebastian's hand reached beneath her shirt. He'd been caught, palm over her breast, dick grinding against her, his mouth on hers.

He remembered his father's yell, her mother coming running, words like statutory rape being flung around them. Next thing he knew, Ashley had been shipped off to boarding school abroad. She hadn't returned. Not for summers or holidays. She'd chosen to stay with friends, and her mother, happy not to have a child to worry about, hadn't cared. She'd even made sure Ashley's boarding school was covered in her divorce agreement, ensuring she didn't come home and disrupt her life.

"Sebastian!" Sierra elbowed him in his side. "Where did your mind go?" she asked him.

"It doesn't matter," he muttered, knowing that it did.

"I guess we should say hello." Nudging him forward, Sierra walked over to Ethan and Ashley, Sebastian beside her.

"Ethan, are you doing okay?" Sierra asked.

"I'm hanging in there. Don't worry about me." Ethan managed a smile and Ashley squeezed his shoulder in a show of silent support.

Sierra glanced up at her. "Hi, Ashley." His sister spoke quietly, with a hint of what might even be embarrassment.

She and Ashley, though the same age, hadn't bonded during Ashley's time at their home. In fact, Sierra had made it a point to exclude the newcomer, worried the pretty girl would be competition for her at home and at school, something she'd admitted later on and felt badly about after Ashley was gone.

"Hi, Sierra. It's good to see you." Ashley tipped her head in acknowledgment, her gaze then falling on his. "Sebastian," she said coolly.

"Ashley." Her name sounded rough in his throat. "I'm surprised to see you."

"Ethan needed me," she said simply, giving nothing of her relationship with his brother away.

It bothered him in ways he couldn't define. The fact that she was here, back after all this time, her hand on his brother's shoulder, their body language telling him their relationship wasn't new.

"I didn't know you two kept in touch," Sebastian

said, hands in the front pockets of his pants.

Ethan narrowed his gaze. "Not now," he said, his tone prohibiting further conversation.

Sebastian narrowed his gaze. That was Ethan, all pronouncement and expecting everyone to fall in line. And though right now, he understood, Sebastian had questions he wanted answers to about the relationship he hadn't known existed between Ethan and Ashley.

She seemed like a friend. A good, solid friend and nothing more, but it bothered him that Ethan had clearly been part of her life—and he hadn't.

He drew a deep breath, knowing that his brother was right and that this wasn't the time or the place for a confrontation. Discretion was important in this room full of people, so for propriety's sake, Sebastian silently backed off, knowing it wasn't the end of the conversation.

AS THE REST of the day passed, painful for everyone involved, Sebastian was acutely aware of Ashley standing by Ethan's side, a strong presence, surprising Sebastian because, as was beginning to become a theme in his life, he'd been in the dark when it came to his own family.

Why hadn't he known Ethan stayed in touch, had a relationship with Ashley after she'd gone? He hadn't thought to ask, never considered why she didn't come back, just accepted the way things were. Because he was a selfish ass, he thought, amazed now that he'd let things just go.

After the funeral, close family and friends returned to Ethan's apartment, where his personal assistant had ordered in food and hired help to serve guests who came back. Hours passed, time during which they remembered Mandy and her smile, her sense of humor.

But finally, by the end of the evening, Ethan told them he wanted nothing more than to be alone. Guests began to file out. The servers left. And considering all the siblings lived in the same luxury high-rise building, it was easy for them to all go their separate ways and retire for the night.

All except for Ashley, who remained in Ethan's apartment.

Aware of her presence on another floor of the building, keenly conscious of her closeness with his brother, the type and depth of the relationship unknown to him, Sebastian pulled out a bottle of Jack and indulged.

✧   ✧   ✧

GOD, SHE'D KILL for some chocolate, Ashley thought, after the last of the company left for the night. It was an indulgence she didn't allow herself often, her mother's words still ringing in her head. Healthy eating, healthy body. And though her mother had watched what she'd eaten because she wanted to look good for her man of the moment, Ashley had internalized her words. She rarely indulged in a chocolate treat because it reminded her of ... Sebastian.

Dammit. She shook her head and pushed him out of her thoughts.

Alone in the living room of Ethan's apartment, she straightened the pillows on the sofa and glanced around. The servers had taken care of the silverware, plates, and glasses, and there wasn't anything left for her to do. So she headed for the kitchen to make sure things were clean for the morning, killing time and giving Ethan more opportunity to be alone.

The day had been rough, as funerals tended to be. For Ashley, she'd had the added stress of dealing with people she hadn't seen in eight years.

Of facing Sebastian.

Despite being prepared, seeing him again had been a shock. When she was younger, he'd been a gorgeous guy, a guy who'd seemed to understand her when no one else bothered to care. Until he hadn't.

Now, over eight years later, he was an extremely sexy man. He'd filled out, his body muscular, evident even beneath his well-cut suit, his dark hair cut short but stylish, and his face was, in her opinion, a work of art. She could stare at him for hours.

Which sucked considering she still resented the hell out of him and for damned good reason.

She'd kept busy throughout the afternoon and evening and managed not to let herself be cornered by him at any point, not that she had the sense he wanted to talk to her. He'd appeared surprised to see her again and definitely puzzled by her relationship with his brother. More than once, she'd caught him staring at her over the top of his tumbler glass, his blue eyes intent as he studied her.

Just looking at him brought her back to the past. She braced both hands against the stainless-steel sink and sighed, remembering his betrayal as if it were yesterday. She might have been the one to come on to him, a teenage girl certain she knew what she wanted, but he hadn't pushed her away. They'd been caught *together* by his father. Yet the next morning, as she'd made her way downstairs, hoping adult tempers had cooled down, she'd heard voices coming from his father's study.

"I think boarding school abroad is the smartest, safest option," Alexander Knight had said. "Ashley will make friends there, and it will take the temptation away from Sebastian." He'd clearly had no problem all but punishing her for *their* mutual actions.

She'd flattened herself against the wall outside the study, where the door was partially open.

"I agree," her mother had said, not in the least bit concerned about sending her daughter away. Ashley had been hurt but not surprised. Jocelyn had probably seen boarding school as a benefit, giving her more spa time, she still thought bitterly. Although she had made peace with her mother, spoke to her occasionally and on holidays, she'd never forgotten the woman hadn't been there for her when Ashley was growing up.

"It's not right," Ethan had said, standing up for Ashley. Being there as he'd been from that day on. "Keep her home and let Sebastian get his shit together."

Alexander, who didn't like to make parental decisions, must have been going around the room, taking advice, because Parker spoke up next. "I don't care," he said. "Do what you think is right."

Switzerland, she thought, even now. It always amused her that though the nickname came originally from his skiing, it fit his placid personality. When it came to family choices, he let things swirl around him, not taking sides.

"Sebastian? You've been silent," his father said.

"Come on," Ethan said. "Keep your dick in your pants and let her stay. She doesn't deserve to be sent away."

Ashley had leaned against the wall outside the study and held her breath, realizing whatever Sebastian said next would determine her fate. She might not love it here, in this big house and new school, but boarding school abroad would be so much worse. Lonelier, she'd thought with a shudder.

"Jesus Christ. You're really going to put this on me?" Sebastian had asked, sounding pissed.

"You're older," Ethan reminded him. "You can control yourself."

"She runs around the house in tight sweats and doesn't wear a bra. I'm only human," Sebastian muttered.

"And that answers that. Discussion closed," Alexander said. "I'll call my contacts abroad and see if I can get her into a good school come September." He paused, then, "Behave yourself for the rest of the summer," he muttered to his son.

To this day, Ashley's stomach lurched when she thought of how they'd discussed her life as if she were a thing to be bounced around without thought or care. All because Sebastian hadn't spoken up. Hadn't said he'd keep his hands to himself so she could stay.

Blowing out a deep breath at the memory, she straightened her shoulders, reminding herself it was in the past. Just because she was here for Ethan now didn't mean she had to deal with Sebastian. That decided, she headed into Ethan's study, where he'd holed up after the apartment emptied out.

She stepped inside to find him staring out the window into the dark night, his thoughts probably on his deceased wife.

"Hey," she said softly.

He turned to face her, deep grooves around his mouth. "I don't know how to thank you. I know what it took for you to come today. To face everyone after all this time."

She swallowed hard. From the moment her fate had been sealed in that study, she hadn't seen any point in coming back. Hadn't considered the Knights family in any way. Until Ethan had shown up on her doorstep at school. He'd been the big brother she'd never had, always a presence in her life, showing up for her in ways no one else ever had.

"There's nothing I wouldn't do for you." She walked over and took his hand. "I'm here for you as long as you need me."

"Thank you," he said. "I have an extra room for you to stay in," he said, gesturing across the apartment.

She shook her head. "I don't want to get in the way." He needed time alone, to grieve. "I made a hotel reservation."

"How long are you in town for?" he asked.

She shrugged. "As long as I feel it's necessary." If

she left it up to him, he'd tell her he was fine. That she didn't need to stay. She knew better. He'd never really lean on other people unless forced to.

Jonathan had called her a few times, but Ashley hadn't answered, not wanting to deal with his persistence about the proposal she'd turned down.

"Look, we have a company-owned apartment in the building, where family and friends stay when they're in town," Ethan said, interrupting her thoughts. "It's fully furnished. You can use it while you're here. Stay here tonight and we'll get you settled in tomorrow. I'll feel better knowing you're close by."

She knew he was throwing that last line out there so she wouldn't argue. "You're not going to take no for an answer, are you?" she asked.

He raised an eyebrow and shook his head. "Nope."

"Okay. I'll stay there."

He managed a smile. "Which brings me to another point." He paused, and she knew, without a doubt, what the topic was going to be. "Cut Sebastian some slack? He was just a kid when things happened between you."

She swallowed hard. "It's complicated, Ethan. It's not just because we were caught making out. I don't blame him for that. We were both young and stupid."

It was what she'd overheard that stayed with her,

even now. How he'd all but thrown her out of the house without thought. But she wasn't about to bother Ethan with the past. Not now.

"Don't worry. I can be civil," she assured him. As long as Sebastian gave her a wide berth, she thought. But to Ethan, she said, "You won't have to worry about me being around your brother." She was here to make Ethan's life easier, not more difficult.

But the playboy wasn't someone she wanted in her life in any form.

Chapter Three

ETHAN HAD INSISTED on going back to work almost immediately, so for the rest of the family and their employees, life went on as usual. Except for Sebastian, who now had to deal with Ashley being around, at the office and at his brother's apartment, a constant fixture, taking care of Ethan.

She brought him homemade muffins and Starbucks in the morning, made sure he ate lunch in the afternoons, and the nights Sebastian or his siblings showed up with dinner for Ethan, Ashley was there, her fitted but obviously expensive dresses hugging her body, her warm vanilla scent permeating the air. If he thought she'd been a temptation when he was younger, she was even more of an enticement now.

Except now she didn't give him the time of day, and it pissed him off. He wasn't a bad guy, and they'd both had a role in getting caught together.

So what was her problem with him?

Not wanting to cause trouble and upset Ethan, he let it go, ignoring the subtle tension for days, until he came back from lunch to hear female laughter. Sierra, who headed the social media division of the company, and Ashley stood together in the break room, drinking from Starbucks cups and laughing over something, big smiles on their faces. They'd obviously broken the ice that had existed between them from the past. Ashley could get over whatever differences she'd had with Sierra.

Just not with him.

Coming on top of his bruised feelings concerning his family's treatment, it hurt. So when Sierra headed for her office, Sebastian rose to his feet and strode to the break room, determined to have it out with Ashley, once and for all.

He stepped into the room as she dumped her coffee cup into the trash. She glanced up, met his gaze, and started to walk around him, in a sudden hurry to leave. His gaze took in her deep purple dress, wound tight around her ample breasts, small waist, and still-enticing ass.

Ignoring his cock, which had definitely taken notice, he cleared his throat. "Ashley."

She froze in the doorway and turned, eyebrows raised as she waited to hear what he had to say.

"This is ridiculous. You, me, this cold war we've got going on." He extended a hand in peace. "What do you say?" He braced himself, ready for the slide of her hand against his skin.

But she ignored the gesture, her eyes frosty, and despite her rebuffing him, he found something sexy about the cool blue stare.

"There's no cold war, Sebastian. I just have nothing to say to you." She drew back her shoulders, the dress pulling tighter over her breasts.

"Are you really holding a grudge over something we both played a role in?" He didn't add that she'd initiated the encounter, that she'd come on to him. He didn't think she'd appreciate the reminder.

A slow smile spread across her glossed lips. "You think that's why I have no desire to engage in small talk? Or have any kind of relationship? No. That's not it." She shook her head. "I can take responsibility for my role in what happened between us. I'm well aware I started things."

"Then—"

She stepped closer, her scent pervading his senses, going right to his dick.

"I was there, Sebastian. I heard what you said to your father in his study. You were the one thing that stood between me being completely cut off from the world I knew. You were eighteen and you didn't step up and say, *hey, I'll behave. Keep Ashley home.* So if you're wondering why I have no use for you, now you know."

He blinked in surprise, her words coming out like a verbal slap. Jesus. All these years, and he'd had no idea she'd been outside that room. Shame filled him as it always did when he remembered that time. In the moment, he hadn't believed his dad would ship Ashley abroad. And when he'd realized his father had been serious about boarding school, he'd gone to the man's study to ask him to change his mind. "Too late, son. Money paid. Nonrefundable. It's a done deal."

"I was young and I fucked up," Sebastian admitted out loud to her, wanting her to know he understood.

She narrowed her gaze. "You sure did. And now I'd appreciate it if you left me alone."

He did his best not to wince or react to her barbed words, instead trying one more time to get past her walls. "It's been eight years," he reminded her. "I'm not the same man I was then."

She raised one eyebrow in disbelief. "Really? From what I understand, your habits regarding women and booze haven't changed much. And frankly, I don't care. I'm just here for Ethan."

He hated the fact that her words had merit, that Ethan had probably clued her in to his partying ways.

He shook his head, knowing there was no way she'd soften. So he opted for the question still nagging at him. "Just what is your relationship with my brother?" he asked.

"He's been my rock," she said simply. "He kept in touch after I was sent away. He made sure I had a semblance of family. Someone to care when I had a birthday or at Christmas."

Jesus, Sebastian thought. And he'd had no fucking clue. Worse, he hadn't given those things a thought.

"So if coming home to help him means I have to deal with you, so be it," Ashley said, unaware of the turmoil rushing through him. "But I'd appreciate it if you'd make it easy for me and keep your distance." And on that statement, she flipped her long blonde hair over her shoulder, a clear dismissal, as she walked past him, head held high.

Fuck.

Even after all this time, she had every right to be pissed at him.

The truth ate away at him until he couldn't focus or sit still in his seat. The appointment he had at three came at an opportune time. He told his secretary he was leaving and headed out of the office, then stopped to pick up Chinese before going home with takeout loaded in a paper bag. The whiskey from the night of the funeral was waiting for him, too.

He ate.

He drank.

He felt like shit, his family's unwillingness to take him seriously, to include him in the important parts of their life, wrecking him. And Ashley's anger, over eight years old but legitimate, twisted in his gut.

He took a healthy sip from the tumbler, forced to look deep and acknowledging at last, in his heart, their characterization of him had merit, no matter that he'd had his reasons.

His mother had died just as he was finishing middle school and entering high school, and they'd been close. He'd confided in her, had fun with her, loved her. Watching her grow frail as cancer ate away at her devastated him. And the fact that his father was never around, that he'd never bothered to hide his affairs – he smelled of perfume when he came home, if he came home at all—made Sebastian angry at the world.

Elizabeth Knight passed away at home and Sebastian reeled, acting out as much and as often as he could. Not even Ethan's calming presence – he'd returned home from Duke University in North Carolina and enrolled at New York University – kept Sebastian in line. He'd made damned sure his father had his hands full bailing him out of trouble. From cheating to skipping class, bailing on school altogether, to drinking and smoking, cigarettes and marijuana, and getting caught, Sebastian had done it all.

And Alexander Knight had had to tap-dance to keep his son in the private school that meant so much to the man. He was on a first-name basis with the cops who brought Sebastian home. A shrink might say Sebastian was looking for attention from his old man, but Sebastian himself thought he just wanted his father to pay. In time, in money, in any way he could for what he'd done to Sebastian's mom.

The years of partying continued through college and business school, but he did take work seriously, had believed he'd stepped up to perform his role in Knight Time Technology. Obviously, though, his siblings didn't see him the same way.

And as he glanced around, he was forced to admit the truth—from the pool table in the middle of the family room to the liquor cabinet, healthily stocked and well used, to the women listed by first names and reminders like *"red everywhere"* noted in his phone—the way he lived backed up Ashley's claim and his family's view of him. He really hadn't changed, and it had taken Mandy's death and Ashley's return to point out that ugly fact.

He glanced at the tumbler in his hand and frowned, throwing it against the wall, watching as it shattered, gold liquid staining the wall and dripping onto the floor.

It was embarrassing, he thought, having lived his life and not realized how his siblings saw him. How Ashley saw him. It was as if he'd been in a bubble, behaving no better than his father, doing what he desired without thought to those around him. Without even caring enough about himself.

Was that what he wanted? To do his job but be a waste of space otherwise?

Hell no, he thought, waking himself up and acknowledging the kind of man he wanted to be. A better man than his father was. A man his brothers could count on, be proud of. A man his sister could turn to for anything and know he'd be there, not out partying or fucking when his family was trying desperately to reach him.

And a man Ashley could look at not with disgust and condemnation but with respect.

SEBASTIAN WOKE UP the next morning, surprisingly clearheaded and ready to deal with the day and the people in his life. Feeling uplifted and determined, he showered and put on his suit because he had scheduled business meetings, and made himself a cup of coffee, downing it before heading downstairs to the convenience store across the street to pick up something important.

Then he walked to the elevator so he could head upstairs to where Ashley now lived.

They needed to have a conversation. One that changed the direction of their relationship. And they would have a relationship, because another thing had become clear to him as he lay in bed last night, trying to fall asleep.

She meant something to him. She always had.

Many women had come and gone from his life and he'd been unable or unwilling to commit. For good reason, he realized now. None had been Ashley. Seeing her again had been the kick in the ass he needed to realize something had been missing from his life, and there was every possibility it was Ashley.

She was someone he genuinely liked and could talk to. Someone he also desired with a passion the likes of which he'd never experienced since their one fateful, heated kiss. He didn't care how young they'd been, he'd wanted her. He still did.

She was the only person he'd ever confided in about his mother's death, his father's infidelities, his problems in school. He remembered sitting up late at night spilling his guts. She'd listened and vice versa. He'd heard her when she'd admitted how much she resented her mother's jumping from wealthy man to wealthy man, how lonely she was in her new home.

If only he hadn't let his dumb hormones lead him around, her life might have been different. He owed her for that. He wanted to make it up to her for pushing her out of what should have been a safe place. For upending her life.

More than that, he wanted to see what could be between them now that they were adults. And to do that, he needed her to see the man he believed he could be. One who was willing to go after what he wanted.

And what he wanted was Ashley.

✧   ✧   ✧

ASHLEY STOOD IN the kitchen, drinking a cup of coffee, waiting for the caffeine to make its way through her system and wake her up. She needed that jolt to get going in the morning. She took another long sip as the doorbell to the new apartment rang. She was still getting used to the place after only a few days, but at least it came with a Keurig.

She placed the mug down on the counter, tightened the sash on her light blue silk robe, and walked to the door, surprised to see Sebastian when she looked through the peephole.

She drew a deep breath and opened the door. "Hi," she said warily, looking into his light blue eyes. She noticed he was dressed for the day at the office in a dark suit, fitting well around his broad shoulders, giving him a sexy, stunning appearance, while she was too aware of how little she was wearing.

"Hi," he said, leaning against the doorframe.

She raised her eyebrows, waiting for him to tell her

what he wanted on her doorstep so early.

Reaching into his pocket, he pulled out a king-size Hershey chocolate bar and extended it between them. She couldn't mistake it for anything but what it was. A reminder of their shared past and a peace offering. He knew her mother hadn't kept chocolate in the house, knew Hershey's was her favorite candy especially *at that time of the month*. He'd sneak her candy bars at night and they'd share one over their late conversations about their parents, life … everything.

He studied her with those intense blue eyes, waiting for a reaction. Despite herself, the corners of her lips twitched in amusement and she grinned.

"Fine. Come in," she said, snagging the candy bar and sashaying back inside, touched and surprised he remembered the small gesture that had meant so much to her once upon a time.

She headed for the living room and he followed her lead. Finally, she reached the sofa and turned to face him.

"I know you want nothing to do with me," he said when he had her attention. "But I have some things I need to say, and I don't want to do it at the office, where we have an audience."

She nodded in understanding.

"Can we sit?" he asked.

She inclined her head and chose a spot on the sofa,

keeping her legs princess style, tucked together and to the side.

But that didn't stop him from staring, his gaze a laser on her exposed skin. She had the urge to shift around, but she couldn't move her legs without exposing her panties beneath. And with his stare hot on her bare calves, she couldn't afford to draw his attention farther up her thighs.

She cleared her throat. "What did you want to talk about?" she asked him as he sat in a chair across from her.

With him dressed impeccably in his suit, looking so handsome and sexy, it was hard for her not to squirm as they stared at each other.

He leaned forward and said, "I gave a lot of thought to what you said yesterday. About what you heard in my father's study and how I didn't stand up for you. How you think I haven't changed." He sounded sober, intense.

She nodded, aware she'd been very hard on him. Hurtfully so. But it had been the first time she'd seen him in years, the first time she was able to express her anger and hurt in his presence. She'd needed to express her bottled-up feelings and she had.

But now she realized she'd probably gone too far. "I shouldn't have mentioned your current behavior. I really don't know you anymore."

She rubbed her palm along the silk of her robe, feeling the soft fabric as a distraction from his large presence. The scent of his cologne had followed him into her apartment, and every time she inhaled, she breathed him in. It was all she could do not to uncross and recross her legs, admitting to her discomfort and awareness.

"Much as it hurts to admit," he said, unaware of his effect on her, "you had valid points. About the past and the present." He met her gaze, his expression contrite but no less handsome for the regret she saw in his face. "I'm sorry, Ashley. For being selfish when we were kids and for you paying the price for my actions. Or lack of action, as the case may be."

She blew out a breath at his unexpected admission and apology, taken off guard and affected by them. What could she say to that? *I still want to hate you? I still blame you?*

Wouldn't that be petty when he'd obviously done a lot of introspection in the last twenty-four hours, taking her words and feelings seriously?

"Thank you," she said instead, finding she meant it more than she would have thought.

"I need you to know, I never thought Dad was going to send you away. And when I heard your mother talking about it with a friend, I went to his study and asked him not to do it." He clenched his hands together as he spoke. "But he'd put it in motion, paid the deposit. I couldn't undo the damage I'd done." He blew out a breath. "The truth is, I was young, selfish, and I let it happen. I'm sorry."

She glanced down at her hand, slowed the nervous movement on the soft fabric. "Thank you for that," she whispered, her voice choked with emotion. She hadn't expected such sincerity from him, such frank self-awareness.

"I'd like a fresh start with you." He spoke earnestly, his husky voice full of what sounded like hope.

Her first impulse, the one coming from the teenager he'd hurt, was to tell him no. She didn't want to trust him now. But the adult inside her understood that people grew up and changed. Had Sebastian?

She really didn't know.

But she couldn't be a bitch to him forever. "Okay. We can start over." They could forge a truce, as adults with people in common. After all, they were tied together by Ethan, if nothing else.

A slow, pleased grin spread across his handsome face, relief mixed with a hint of intriguing mischievousness she didn't trust. A sensual look in his gaze that made her very afraid she wasn't agreeing for Ethan's sake but for her own.

Because there was still something very compelling about Sebastian Knight.

✧　✧　✧

ASHLEY ADJUSTED TO the pace of New York City easier than she'd thought she would, finding herself enjoying being back in the United States. In the beginning, she kept busy enough baking for Ethan, bringing him his favorite cranberry muffins each morning along with fresh Starbucks at the office and helping him clean out Mandy's things, something he asked her to handle. He didn't want to deal with her clothing or personal effects, requesting only that she save the photographs and things Ashley thought might have had meaning to Mandy.

Ashley donated a lot of items to women's shelters and Goodwill, using the time to make conscious choices about where Mandy's things would do the most good. To her surprise, she wasn't as bored as she'd have thought not working at her day job, from which she'd taken a leave of absence.

As a forensic accountant, she was basically a fraud investigator, digging into accounts and researching where people hid money. She was good with numbers, liked being busy, and spent her days looking to prove insurance fraud, among other things. Since she'd rarely taken vacation days, she appreciated the time off now.

The apartment Ethan had offered up for her to stay in was immaculate, comfortable, well-decorated, and on another floor from Sebastian. Even after his apology, she'd expected to see an array of women coming and going, especially on the weekends, but since his visit, it had been quiet, making her think maybe that part of him had changed.

She wished she could say she didn't think about him but she did. Too often. He was too much a sexual presence for her to pretend he didn't affect her, yet she managed to keep her distance, and that was what she knew she needed.

✧ ✧ ✧

SEBASTIAN DIDN'T APPRECIATE being summoned by Ethan, but he strode into his office anyway, surprised to find Ashley already there.

Her soft hair fell over her shoulders, her beautiful profile relaxed. Because she didn't know he was there.

"What's with the summons?" he asked his brother.

She swung around, obviously surprised to see him.

"You, sit, too," Ethan said.

The fact that he was used to Ethan's demanding personality didn't lessen the annoyance he felt. "I don't appreciate the commands," he muttered, but sat in a chair anyway.

"Ethan? What's going on?" Ashley asked, sounding confused.

"I'm still waiting on Parker, but while I have you two, I have something to say."

Ashley leaned forward in her seat. Sebastian leaned back, waiting.

"You're both driving me fucking insane." Ethan held up a hand before they could speak. "I know you both mean well, I know you're worried about me, but I can't take the hovering."

He glanced at Sebastian. "I don't need my hand held at every meeting. I don't need my mail delivered by you, as an excuse to check up on me every damned day." He turned to Ashley. "And I'm sick to death of cranberry muffins."

"I could make blueberry," she offered, tongue in cheek.

Sebastian grinned. She met his gaze, her soft lips lifting as they shared their first joint chuckle in what felt like forever, and it felt good.

But he hadn't realized he'd been smothering his brother. He'd just been worried about him, as Ethan had said.

"I need space." Ethan looked at Ashley. "Do you plan on going back to London soon?" he asked, his voice gentle.

Sebastian held his breath, waiting for an answer, not ready for her to leave. Not when he hadn't had a chance to spend time with her, to make headway, showing her the man he really was.

"Honestly? I'm not ready to leave you alone," she

said to Ethan, and Sebastian blew out a relieved breath. "I know you have your family around you, but I feel like it's so soon, and I want to be here for you."

His expression softened at her admission. "You know I appreciate everything. Both of you."

"Sorry I'm late," Parker interrupted, joining them then, walking in without knocking.

Sebastian wondered why they were all gathered here as Ethan acknowledged Parker with a nod.

"Now that we're all here, I need to let you know about what's going on with our San Francisco office and Keystone project on which they've been working."

Sebastian knew they'd won a bid to provide the high-tech locks on all the doors for Keystone, a multimillion-dollar defense contractor, building a new, secure headquarters building in northern California. As far as Sebastian knew, things had been progressing as planned.

Ethan glanced at Sebastian, letting him know without words that he was deliberately including him, trusting him, making up for what he hadn't done when it came to Mandy.

Sebastian swallowed hard. "What's going on?"

"Of all the stupid shit that can go wrong, the electronic door locks aren't closing securely. The prototypes worked fine, but once installed, they're failing. One piece in the automation is screwing with the entire thing. The whole campus relies on that security. We need to throw money at the problem to determine what's going wrong, but there's no extra money to be found. And we all know Mandy had been running that project."

For six months, Mandy had gone back and forth from New York to California, even living there part time while the project got up and running. She and Ethan had been bicoastal, but it seemed to work for them.

"What I don't know is where Mandy got the money for her drugs. Now there's money missing from the Keystone project. Coincidence? I don't think so. I was blind because I needed to trust her or I had no marriage. And I missed the fact that something was going on right under my nose." Ethan set his jaw tight, clearly tense and pissed off.

"Shit," Parker muttered. "What's the plan?"

Ethan met Parker's gaze. "I'm going to stay on the software people." The keys weren't physical, per se, but used via a smartphone or special key configured to wirelessly perform the opening and closing process. But there were also mechanical parts, and those had been purchased via the California office.

"I want you and Ashley to head out to San Francisco," Ethan continued. "Figure out which parts aren't working in the damn locks. Ashley, you can dig through accounting and Parker, you can calm Stephan Romano, who's losing his fucking mind. We can't afford to lose this project. Our reputation will take a hit, and financially it'll kill us."

"You want me to look at the books?" she asked, sounding surprised. "I thought after I turned down your offer to come work here after I graduated, you handed things over to your friend's firm."

Sebastian's gaze grew wide. Ethan had offered her a job? She could have been back here much sooner? Damn.

"I don't hold grudges," he told her. "Besides, I need you. I don't want anyone getting wind of the fact that we're having problems with such a lucrative project. I trust you," he said gruffly.

She nodded in understanding. "Of course I'll help."

"When do we have to leave?" Parker asked.

Parker, who'd never been meant to have a desk job. He'd been a skiing phenomenon, destined for the Olympics until he tore his ACL on a downhill run and did permanent damage to his knee. Sebastian often did a double take when he walked in here and saw his middle brother in a suit and tie. Parker was a man more comfortable in the outdoors than in the office. He knew the pain his brother felt at being forced into a role he'd never wanted.

Sebastian looked from Ashley to Parker, not surprised that Ethan had chosen Parker to go out and handle Romano. Sebastian had begun to realize they'd put him on deals that were already secure, the lack of trust permeating through his placements in ways he hadn't recognized until now.

"I'll go," Sebastian said, recognizing that this was his chance. The opportunity to show his family he could step up and handle a crisis. Be the man they could rely on.

Beside him, he felt more than saw Ashley stiffen. Going away with him was not in her plans, he thought wryly. But he focused on Ethan, meeting his brother's gaze, not blinking, not wavering.

He wanted this. Not only because it meant spending time with Ashley but because he needed to prove to everyone, including himself, that he could be trusted.

Ethan's gaze slid to Parker, who merely shrugged. "Whatever you decide is fine with me."

Parker's easygoing demeanor stemmed not only from the fact that he was the middle child, who found it easy to let the chaos of four siblings go on around him, but from the fact that he'd come into this business as a last resort and was willing to do what he was told.

Ethan studied Sebastian, thinking about who knew what, holding Sebastian's fate in his hand, before nodding. "Fine. You two leave tomorrow."

Sebastian blew out the breath he'd been holding, before turning to Ashley with what was a deliberately sexy grin on his face. This might be business and it was important, but so was she. And he had no issues mixing business with a bit of pleasure.

Chapter Four

ASHLEY FOUND HERSELF on an evening trip via private jet to San Francisco with Sebastian, totally taken off guard by the sudden turn of events. She hadn't expected to do any work for Knight Time Technology while she was here and certainly hadn't anticipated being sent on a business trip with Sebastian.

During the discussion in Ethan's office, she'd sensed the tension between the brothers when Ethan had ordered Parker to go with her to San Francisco. It seemed to go deeper than just the fact that Sebastian had wanted to be the one to go away with Ashley, although his last dizzying look at her had made that point loud and clear.

Yet here she was, on a private jet, something she'd never flown in before. The luxury was addicting, she mused. There was no comparison of the sheer space on the plane compared to flying commercial. Not even first class could equate to the cozy leather lounge chairs, the mahogany tabletops, the stocked bar, and the flight attendant who knew when to make herself scarce.

She glanced out the window and into the night sky, overwhelmed by the darkness. Inside the plane, the yellow glow of lights illuminated the as she settled in for takeoff, Sebastian beside her.

He seemed preoccupied, and after takeoff, he took out his laptop, keeping busy, tapping away, probably making preparations and setting up meetings for tomorrow at the office. She held her iPad in her hands as they sat in comfortable silence, which she was happy to let go on. With a six-plus-hour flight ahead of them, she wanted to keep things peaceful between them.

A little while after the plane leveled out, Sebastian excused himself to go to the restroom, and Ashley focused on her iPad, checking email and texting her friend Nicole in London. The time difference made it difficult to talk at the same time, so she just checked in, knowing she'd hear back from her tomorrow.

When the ding of a text message sounded, it took her by surprise. It was one a.m. in London and she hadn't expected an answer. She'd just wanted to drop a note to say hello. She opened the message app, surprised to see Jonathan's name pop up on the screen.

Are you there?

She bit down on the inside of her cheek, not really

wanting to answer. She'd been avoiding returning his calls, having realized his persistence in trying to reach her meant he probably hadn't taken the no to his marriage proposal seriously.

Not to mention, the texts from her friends who'd heard from him that she'd turned him down informed her that they thought she was crazy. He was a catch, they said. He obviously loved her, he could give her a good life ... blah, blah, blah. She knew all those things, and they hadn't changed her mind about turning him down.

She blew out a breath and wrote him back, knowing she couldn't avoid it much longer. *I'm here. Busy with family and helping out with the business.* In other words, she wasn't planning on returning just yet.

Oh. I was hoping to hear you were wrapping things up there... I miss you.

"Oh damn," she muttered. "Why are some men so stubborn?" she asked aloud.

"Should I be offended?" Sebastian's deep voice sounded from behind her. "Disparaging my sex?"

She laughed at that. "If the shoe fits..."

He leaned down, looking over her shoulder, his body heat permeating her skin, the warm, male scent of him arousing her senses.

She squirmed in her seat, her nipples hardening at his mere closeness. She smelled his delicious scent; she felt him hovering over her. It had been so long since she'd been sexually affected by a man this way, it was all she could do not to moan in her seat.

"Who is Jonathan?" he asked, taking her off guard.

She flipped her iPad over so he couldn't read her personal texts. "None of your business." His words drew her out of the haze she'd allowed herself to indulge in.

"He obviously misses you. Is he someone you were seeing back in London?" Sebastian asked, an edge in his voice as he pushed for an answer.

She curled her fingers around the device, well aware he hadn't moved, was still leaning over her, hovering in her personal space.

The iPad dinged again.

"Come on, turn it over. See what lover boy wants."

With a frown, and curious herself, she flipped the tablet. *Come home so we can work things out.*

"Pushy SOB," Sebastian muttered.

"You don't even know him. He's a perfectly nice man." She found herself defending Jonathan, even as she did her best not to wince at the pathetic way her description of him sounded. Unfortunately it was true. Jonathan was a perfectly pleasant man.

Behind her, Sebastian snickered. "I suppose the sex is perfectly *nice*, too."

She couldn't believe he'd go there. Of all the nerve!

She jumped up from her seat, leaving her iPad on the table, while he walked around, meeting her face-to-face in the aisle.

"Problem?" he asked, an amused smile on his too handsome face.

She settled her hands on her hips, not willing to let him make fun of her. "Sex isn't everything in a relationship. There are other things that are more important."

He raised an eyebrow, obviously surprised at her pronouncement. "Like what?" He stepped closer, invading her space, his delicious scent almost a part of her.

She hesitated and he jumped on her reticence. "Tell me, Ashley, what's more important between a couple than sex?"

Her mouth ran dry but she managed to answer. "Shared interests, kindness, understanding."

"But not sex?" His eyebrows raised high. "You're telling me it doesn't matter to you if a man turns you on? If just being with him makes your panties wet?" His voice grew deeper, huskier. "If just looking at him makes your nipples turn hard, like yours are now?"

She refused to glance down and see that he was right. She already felt the dampness between her legs, the slick pulsing of her sex. Just from being near Sebastian. She swallowed hard.

"Tell me, Ashley, does lover boy have you panting like I did eight years ago?" He paused, then, "When he sticks his tongue into your mouth, do you find yourself rubbing your breasts against his chest? Your pussy into his thigh?"

He reached up and ran his thumb across her damp lower lip. "Does he make you breathe as heavily as you are now?" His face was now inches from hers, his eyes darkened with desire. "Are you really telling me *this* isn't important?" His thumb pressed deeper into her lip, need filling her more with every breath.

She couldn't answer him. Couldn't deny his words. Not when she wanted him down to the very depths of her soul.

He leaned in slowly, giving her every opportunity to push him away or to walk away herself. Except she didn't. She remained in place, her lips hovering near his.

She didn't know who moved first. Couldn't say and didn't care. Because in a heartbeat, his mouth was on hers. Tasting. Devouring. Reminding her that when the yearning was mutual, sex *was* important, and in this moment, that desire blocked out every rational thought that tried to break through and remind her of why being with Sebastian this way was a very bad idea.

His tongue swept into her mouth, tangling with hers, a delicious counterpoint to the throbbing between her legs, as she kissed him back, all hesitance, all thoughts gone but one.

She wanted him.

She raised her hands, wrapping her arms around his shoulders while his palms had settled firmly on her hips, holding her in place for a kiss that was more like a feasting.

He tasted delicious, all man and Sebastian, his mouth firmly on hers, telling her he was in charge.

And in this moment, she liked it that way. She wanted him to take her out of her head, to show her the pleasure she'd claimed meant nothing, the gratification she'd wanted to deny.

Instead she lost herself to the sweep of his tongue, the bite of his teeth on her lip, the suction of his kisses as his mouth moved over her cheek and along her jaw. She moaned at the sensual assault, lost in the way he made her feel.

He nibbled down her neck, sucking on her collarbone until she was a trembling mess in his arms. Only the firm grip of his arm, which had, at some point, moved around her waist, held her jelly-like legs up at all.

Suddenly he lifted his head, meeting her gaze, his blue eyes a deeper than normal shade. "Think about *that* when you remember the perfectly *nice* guy waiting for you in London." He set her firmly on her feet, waited until she was steady, until she could hold herself up without the dizzying assault on her senses affecting her.

Only then did he stride over to the bar and pour himself a glass of whiskey. Taking a sip, he met her gaze and held her stare, desire still pulsing between them.

God, the man was frustratingly smug and extremely potent. And what was she thinking? Just out of one relationship, letting a man she'd just barely forgiven nearly give her an orgasm midair without even touching her?

His grin drove her insane, and she tore her gaze away and walked to her seat, sitting down, all too aware of her soaked underwear, the desire he'd awakened remaining alive inside her.

She tried to focus on her tablet, pulling up a book to read, but the words swirled together on the page.

She didn't know whether to be embarrassed at how easily she'd fallen apart in his arms, angry at him for kissing her, or annoyed with herself for allowing it. After all, he'd given her the opportunity to walk away. She hadn't. She'd let him goad her into that kiss.

Gah!

He spilled out the remainder of his drink and walked back to his seat beside her, sitting down, picking up his laptop, and going back to work. But not before glancing her way and treating her to a wink and a sinful smile, the dimple in his cheek she'd been ignoring since her return coming out to play.

One she was afraid, if alone with him for any period of time, she wouldn't be able to resist.

✧   ✧   ✧

KISSING ASHLEY HADN'T been on Sebastian's agenda when he'd walked onto the plane. Convincing her she could trust him again had been. But Sebastian didn't do competition well, probably because women had always come easy to him. To hear that Ashley had a man waiting for her burned in his gut. Jealousy was an unfamiliar emotion, but it had swept over him completely. All he'd been able to think about, to do, was give her something to compare and contrast to that asshole nice guy back in London.

Now he was possessed by the feel of her in his arms, the warm scent of her skin, and the luscious taste of her lips. But he couldn't forget that he had a job to do. One that was important not just to him personally but to his entire family professionally. The business had been started by his great-great-grandfather, and Sebastian refused to have their biggest contract end because he couldn't fix things here. Shifting his focus wouldn't be easy, but he knew how to compartmentalize when he needed to.

They arrived at the luxury hotel near their company's San Francisco office close to midnight Pacific time, and the woman behind the desk checked them in.

"Your company suite is ready for you, Mr. Knight," she said. "How many keys would you like?"

"Two," Sebastian said.

"Wait, what do you mean, company suite? I want my own room," Ashley said, leaning against the counter.

The brunette helping them shook her head. "I'm sorry but we're all booked. There are two bedrooms in the suite, however." She glanced between Ashley and Sebastian, obviously anxious that she couldn't please them both.

"Excuse us a minute." He took Ashley's arm and pulled her aside, beneath a large fake tree in the lobby. "We're adults, Ashley. You'll have your own room. In the suite. Can we just get settled? We've been traveling all night, and I don't know about you but I'm beat." Tiredness had seeped into his bones, a dull throb settling in the base of his skull.

She frowned, obviously not happy.

"Come on. It can't be a hardship for you to share a suite with me. I mean, I've already apologized for the past. We made peace."

"Then you kissed me on the plane," she hissed.

He raised an eyebrow at the accusation. "Can you really say I kissed you? I mean, was it crystal clear who made that ultimate move?"

Her gaze narrowed even more, but he shook his head, knowing he was right. "I'll control myself," he promised. It was the best he could do to get her to agree to the sleeping arrangements. He doubted she'd be happy on a couch in the lobby of the hotel.

"Even if I prance around in tight sweats and no bra?" she tossed back at him.

Really? She was going there? "I'm a grown man," he assured her, through gritted teeth. "I can keep my hands to myself." He raised both palms in the air in a promise he knew he'd hate to have to keep.

And after her response to him on the plane, he knew he shouldn't have to. But the next move clearly wouldn't be his, he thought, wondering if she had the guts to step up and act on her desire.

"And that's what you should have said back when your father asked you," she muttered, her arms folded across her chest.

It was his turn to frown at the fact that she couldn't just let it go. "Last I heard, when you accepted an apology, you left the past where it belongs. In the past."

Her sexy lips pushed out in a pout, but her next words belied her expression. "You're right. So fine to the suite. I can be an adult, too," she said on a sigh.

He chalked her argumentative behavior up to exhaustion, and with that settled, he strode back to the desk clerk and completed their registration, handing Ashley a key card.

Exhausted, they made their way to the twelfth floor and walked to the end of a long hallway, where Sebastian let them into the suite.

A few minutes later, a bellman delivered their luggage and, at Ashley's direction, put her bag in one room and Sebastian's luggage in another.

Sebastian tipped the man and he walked out.

"I'm tired," she said, meeting his gaze. "I'm going to turn in. What time do you want to get going in the morning?"

"I'll order room service. We can eat here and leave by eight thirty. We're just a few blocks from the office. We'll be there by nine."

She nodded and closed herself in her room, leaving him to stew over the fact that she'd rebuilt her walls after that kiss, making them even higher than they'd been before. It pissed him off, because not only had that kiss been mutual, it'd been the hottest fucking thing he'd ever experienced. And that was saying something.

✧   ✧   ✧

ASHLEY WOKE UP, showered, and readied for the day, choosing a dress, knowing she'd be doing business at the Knight Time Technology offices. She put on makeup and stalled for time, embarrassed to go out to the suite and deal with Sebastian after her little tantrum in the lobby last night. She'd been exhausted, thrown off guard by the kiss, and upset with herself for wanting to pick up where they'd left off as soon as they'd arrived at the hotel. Sharing space would only make keeping her distance more difficult, and she'd taken the surprise circumstances out on him.

She walked out of the room and found him sitting on the terrace drinking a cup of coffee and reading something on his iPad. Breakfast, in a variety of silver-covered plates, awaited her.

She gingerly joined him, clearing her throat when he didn't look up right away. "Good morning," she said.

He put his cup down on the table and rose as she lowered herself into her seat, sitting when she did. "Hi."

The scent of baked goods and waffles or pancakes permeated her senses. The sun shone overhead with a coating of light fog disturbing her view. But a glance over the terrace showed her the city of San Francisco, buildings and curved streets in the distance.

"Hungry?" he asked.

Her stomach grumbled and she grinned. "Starving."

She reached over and poured herself a glass of orange juice, taking a fortifying sip before speaking what she'd rehearsed in the shower. "I'm sorry about last night," she said. "I was just taken off guard by the one-suite arrangement, and I got snippy. I know you already apologized and I won't bring the past up again."

"I appreciate that." He met her gaze, warm blue eyes staring back at her. "Pancakes and bacon?" He was obviously as eager as she to put last night behind them, for which she was grateful.

He lifted the silver tray cover, revealing her guess had been correct. She wasn't about to deny her rumbling belly despite her mother's words always lingering in her head. Ashley's normal breakfast of Greek yogurt, strawberries, and granola didn't hold a candle to the feast in front of her.

"God, yes. I haven't had a decadent breakfast like this in forever." She allowed him to pile her plate full of food and pass over the maple syrup. "You're going to make me fat," she muttered.

"Nothing wrong with indulging," he said, his knowing gaze on hers. "You'll still capture the eye of any man who looks."

She flushed at the compliment, secretly pleased by

his words. But on the other side of them was the fact that he obviously remembered her mother's not-so-subtle chiding whenever she would go for the more fattening foods their housekeeper and cook served. He'd always been there, sneaking her Hershey bars, encouraging her to enjoy her life.

She cut a piece of pancake now drowned in syrup and put it into her mouth, groaning at the delicious taste. His eyes darkened at the clearly sensual sound coming out of her mouth, causing her to squirm in her seat. He might have promised to keep his hands to himself, but that didn't mean she wanted him to, she admitted to herself, the kiss still at the forefront of her mind.

But they were here for business, and it was best she focus on that. "I know your company is all high tech now, but I once heard Ethan talking about your great-great-grandfather having started the business."

Sebastian, still drinking his coffee, nodded. "Rumor has it, and I have no idea if it's true or not, that our great-great-grandfather was a master locksmith." His sexy lips curved upward in a smile as he went on. "They say he was responsible for breaking Billy the Kid out of jail. Personally, I always thought it was an old wives' tale. But it makes for good business conversation when we're trying to close a deal."

She laughed. "It certainly does."

"It also explains why, despite our cyber focus now, we still have a key on our logo. Makes it more relatable to people, too."

She nodded, familiar with their navy Knight Technology logo.

"The company history makes it all the more ironic that we have a multimillion-dollar smart campus deal at stake and we can't get the damned locks to close." Sebastian, furrows in his forehead, frowned. "Great-Great-Grandpa is probably rolling in his grave," he said, sounding frustrated and upset.

"You and your brothers are so dedicated to the business." She knew Ethan lived and breathed it, even when Mandy had been alive.

"Well, Ethan and I are dedicated. So is Parker, but he fell into it because he had no choice. I feel bad he never accomplished his Olympic skiing dreams. Damned accident."

She remembered that time vividly. Ethan had canceled a trip to visit her right after Parker's injury. "It happened while I was abroad, but Ethan told me what was going on."

Sebastian studied her, his expression serious. "Was it bad? Boarding school?"

She sucked in a surprised breath at the question, giving it serious thought. "It was lonely at first." She parsed her words carefully, so as not to make him feel worse than he already did for being the reason she had been sent away. "But eventually I made friends." She pushed the orange juice aside and moved on to pouring herself coffee. It was time for caffeine.

His phone rang then and he glanced down. "The office," he said, his attention now distracted, for which she was grateful.

She didn't know if there would come a time when she'd want to confide in Sebastian about her years away, but now wasn't the time. The past had defined the woman she'd become, and she wasn't ready to delve into that this morning.

Sebastian ended the call and met her gaze. "That was Kyle Elliott, one of the executives at our San Fran office. He wanted to let me know he'd sent a memo, gathering the top people for my meeting this morning."

Ashley nodded. "What do you want me to do?"

"Hit up Accounting. They know to turn over everything and anything that you need to reconcile purchases and receipts. Whatever you ask for should be at your disposal. Talk to the head people in the accounting department. See what you can glean from them."

She patted her lips with a napkin, a move not lost on Sebastian despite the seriousness of the business discussion at hand. His deep blue gaze followed her movement, including the swipe of her tongue over her lips to dampen them.

They might be here on business, might have serious work to do, but nothing personal between them had been settled. At all.

Chapter Five

S EBASTIAN GATHERED THE executives in the San Francisco office and met up with them in the conference room. The meeting was a bust, every executive from each department swearing they did their jobs, nobody stepping up and taking responsibility for the issues the company was having at Keystone.

He then broke them into smaller groups and even talked to them individually, but he got nowhere. Nobody had a clue why the locks weren't closing correctly when the prototypes had worked fine.

At the end of the day, Sebastian leaned against the back seat of the limo, feeling defeated as he pulled on his tie to loosen the noose from around his neck.

"Bad day?" Ashley asked him, settling in beside him, the scent of her perfume the first thing he'd noticed when she'd climbed in and slid into her seat.

"Frustrating as all hell," he muttered. "I got nowhere. I met with the executives in a group and one at a time, and no one has an inkling why our one key part is failing."

Surprising him, she reached out and placed her hand over his, the soft feel of her skin relaxing him and easing his tension.

"To make matters worse, I've been trying to reach Stephan Romano to reassure him I'm here and taking over, but so far he's not returning my calls," he said of their eccentric client, the CEO of Keystone. "How did *you* make out today?" He turned to face her, hoping she'd had more luck than he had in figuring out what was wrong at the company.

She pursed those soft lips, causing him to stifle a groan at the sight of the slight pucker.

"I didn't find anything out of the ordinary, not at a one-day glance. If the company bought something, it was billed and paid for; if they sold, it was invoiced and accounted for. Everything on the project lined up, as far as I could see." She shrugged her shoulders, obviously as at a loss as he was.

"Dammit." He curled his hand into a fist beneath hers.

She smoothed her palm over his, forcing him to unclench and relax. Intertwining their fingers together, she ran her thumb back and forth over his hand in a soothing motion. After last night, he was surprised she was reaching out physically, even if it was just because she was trying to quell his frustration. But he appreciated the gesture, his body responding despite the nonsexual nature of her touch, his cock thickening inside his pants.

"I did spend time with Katherine Downing in Purchasing," Ashley said, unaware of his reaction. "She's the one who got me the receipts and bills I needed. She was helpful with everything I asked for but didn't seem all that keen on talking."

"Hmm. We're going to need a new strategy."

She murmured in agreement, "I'll definitely have to meet with her again. But you know ... I was just thinking. You've been talking to all the high-level execs, but the real day-to-day dealings go on with the lower echelon of employees. Maybe you need to have a meeting with them."

He raised an eyebrow at her suggestion, impressed. "Not a bad idea," he mused. "In the meantime, what do you want to do for dinner?" he asked. "We can stop anywhere."

She glanced out the tinted window as the car wound through the city streets, her long blonde hair falling over her shoulders. His fingers itched to wind themselves in the long strands, but despite her warmth tonight, he didn't act on the impulse.

"I'm really not in the mood to sit down in a restaurant and eat a long, drawn-out dinner. Are you?"

"Hell no." He thought about possibilities, then had an idea. Leaning forward, he spoke to the driver. "First pizzeria you see, stop, please?"

"What are you doing? Bringing food back to the hotel room?" she asked.

He turned to her and grinned. "We're going to drive through the city, share a pizza, and just relax."

Her eyes widened in definite approval. "Oh, that sounds wonderful." She immediately kicked off her heels and stretched out her legs, wriggling her now free toes, drawing his attention to those long legs. "God," she murmured in a husky voice. "I didn't realize how much my feet hurt until I took these off."

He glanced at the high heels, knew she was in pain, and scowled. "I don't get why women wear these things if they're so uncomfortable."

A smirk lifted her lips. "Are you telling me I didn't see you staring at my legs in these spiked heels?"

Caught, he thought with a grin. "I didn't say *I* didn't like them." His gaze drifted down her legs again, deliberately staring at the exposed skin, hoping he was making her squirm.

Before she could react, the car came to a stop.

"Pizza place on the left," the driver said to Sebastian, interrupting their banter-like conversation.

He knew it was safer that way. Better he hopped out now, before he acted on his baser impulses when it came to Ashley.

"I'll be back," he said, his voice a notch lower than usual.

✧   ✧   ✧

HALF AN HOUR later, they had pizza, paper plates, napkins, and bottles of soda spread across the seat. The divider between the front and the passengers had been raised, giving them privacy, the chauffeur having been instructed to just drive. Instrumental music Ashley didn't recognize played low in the background.

She ate without self-consciousness, devouring two slices of large plain pizza, sipping Diet Coke from the bottle, and laughing with Sebastian over anything and everything, their conversation easy and fun. He'd collected the plate and piled the box and garbage onto the floor at his feet for cleaning up later.

He glanced at her and patted his thighs. "Put your feet up here," he said, surprising her.

She narrowed her gaze, hesitantly raising her legs and laying her bare feet in his lap. He wrapped a hand around one foot and began to massage it. Clearly he hadn't forgotten her complaint about pain.

He pressed his thumb into her arch, and she moaned out loud, the incredible feel of him working his fingers into her sore muscles delicious. And extremely arousing. With every press of the pads of his fingers, her sex pulsed with desire, wetness coating her panties. She doubted that had been his intent, but she also knew he wouldn't complain if he knew his massage was turning her on.

He worked her muscles in silence, music light and airy around them, allowing her to close her eyes and focus on the luxurious feel of his touch.

"Feel good?" he asked in a roughened voice, letting her know he was just as affected by this moment as she was.

"Mmm. Incredible."

He worked up her arch and into the skin below her toes, moving upward. She wasn't ticklish. Instead she found the pull on each toe a balm to her pain.

He switched to the other foot, giving it the same treatment until she was heady with the sensations he was creating inside her. His talented hands slid the opposite direction, down her foot to her ankle, kneading the muscles in her calves and moving slowly up her leg, not skimping on the actual massage. He wasn't copping a feel, he was working her muscles, and she appreciated every kneading sensation into her skin.

His fingertips slid up the sensitive point behind her knee, slowly traveling higher and higher still, as if testing her approval. She knew where he was headed, those fingers inching ever closer to the place between her thighs that throbbed with need. Her clit pulsed, the desire for his touch there a tangible thing.

Suddenly he stopped, his hand freezing, fingers wrapped around her thigh.

"What's wrong?" she asked, opening her eyelids

and meeting his serious gaze.

"I said I could keep my hands to myself and I meant it." He released her, and she felt the loss of his warmth against her skin.

Disappointment filled her along with innate understanding. This had to be her choice, her decision. He didn't want to seduce her into a yes that she'd regret later or have her agree in a haze of desire that left her incapable of true consent. They'd been through too much for that. She couldn't deny how much she wanted him and wouldn't lie to herself about that.

But there were other factors to consider before entering into any kind of relationship with Sebastian, including a purely sexual one. She had a life in London, friends there, a job she'd have to go back to. She was only here temporarily, but wasn't that all Sebastian wanted in life? Ethan had told her he had a habit of entering physical relationships that meant nothing to him in the long run. And as for Jonathan, he might not be willing to take no for an answer, but she'd already declined his proposal. He wasn't an obstacle to anything she did with Sebastian.

Ashley realized whatever she said now would set the course of where they went from here. While she was in town.

Did she really want to walk away from this kind of once-in-a-lifetime passion?

She drew a deep breath and faced him. "I don't want you to keep your hands to yourself, Sebastian. Not anymore."

He remained still, listening to her words, and so she continued. "Back then, we were kids and I understand that everyone shared a role in sending me away. I don't blame you, despite me bringing it up again last night. But we're adults now. I swear to you I've put it in the past," she said, hopefully clearing the way to a sexual future between them. She promised herself and silently him, she wouldn't bring up that time in their lives again.

His intent gaze bored into hers. "I believe you," he said. "But I need to hear you say the words. Tell me what you want, Ashley."

It was all up to her.

"You," she whispered. "I want you."

His fingers clenched around her so tightly he'd leave marks. And she didn't care. Then he began to move again, gliding his fingertips up her thighs, no longer focused on massage, clearly on a mission of a different kind. And whereas before, she'd closed her eyes to better enjoy the perks of his massage, now she watched as he pleasured her.

His strong jaw was taut, muscles set as his gaze focused on his fingers, darker and more tanned against her fairer flesh. He slid her dress higher and higher still, crinkling the material above her thighs, revealing her barely there, sexy panties, white lace with a black bow on top. His thumb skimmed along the crease in her thigh, and she gasped, the sensation so intimate, her juices dampened her underwear even more.

"So wet," he murmured. "So turned on." He dipped a finger beneath the bow, the pad of the strong digit gliding over her pubic bone, drifting lower.

"Sebastian." She barely recognized her own deeply husky voice.

"Shh. Let me play."

He removed his hand and pulled her panties down her legs, not taking them off completely. Just slid them down enough to bare her pussy and, at his urging, bend her knee to the side, opening herself wide for him.

"So beautiful." His dark gaze stared at her bared and open intimate flesh. Damp and glistening, she knew.

Her cheeks burned at his perusal, but when his fingers slid over the lips of her sex, parting her and beginning to work her over, she forgot to be embarrassed. Instead she was consumed with the pleasure of his touch.

Gliding back and forth, he slicked her moisture over her bare lips and coated his fingers with her wetness. She writhed beneath him, bucking at his sensual touch and exploration until he placed his palm against her belly, holding her in place.

She groaned at the feeling of possession he invoked, then one finger slid inside her, and at the sudden invasion, her inner walls clasped around him.

"You're tight, baby. You're going to feel so good on my cock."

Her insides spasmed at his bold words.

Releasing his hold on her stomach, he slid his hand lower, his thumb pressing on her clit, drawing circles that her hips began to mimic as she climbed toward an explosive climax.

He circled her clit harder and harder, urging her along with his sex-roughened voice. "Reach for it, baby. Come on." She arched her hips. He pinched her clit. And she cried out, consumed with pleasure, lost in a long spiral that took her over and left her spent and shaking.

She came to herself, her panties around her calves, Sebastian's hand petting her sex, his gaze hot on hers. And his cock throbbing insistently against her legs in his lap.

"Hey," he said, a pleased grin on his face.

"What a way to tour San Francisco," she said.

He burst out laughing before helping her shimmy back into her underwear.

✦   ✦   ✦

SEBASTIAN WATCHED AS Ashley pulled herself together, lowering her dress and sitting up, his own body still on edge from the pleasure he'd provided her. Shaken by the enjoyment he'd gotten from giving her a climax that clearly rocked her world. He was all about tit for tat, giving and receiving during sex, because it was the gentlemanly thing to do. The obligatory thing to do. But there'd been nothing forced about his need to make Ashley come.

What had started as easing her foot pain had become a compulsion. A need to touch and possess her in the most intimate of places. But not one that had blocked out rational thought – he'd needed her permission, needed her approval after all they'd been through before.

But once she'd given him the green light? Touching her had been as necessary to him as breathing. Watching her come had given him as much pleasure as his own orgasm ever had.

When she reached for the waistband of his pants, she startled him, and he grabbed her wrists, stopping her. "No."

"No?" she asked, sounding surprised.

He shook his head. "We have a complicated history, you and I. And this? This was about me giving something to you. Not taking anything back in return."

Holy shit. Who was he and what had happened to his usual MO? Sebastian wondered. In and out. One and done. Mutual sexual acts before moving on ... unless the woman he was with understood there was no future to be had.

Because none had been Ashley.

Shit.

He didn't want her hand on his cock because he needed to fucking think about what he wanted from her. From them.

Before she could reply, her cell phone, which she'd left on the seat of the car, began to ring.

He glanced at the piece of equipment, annoyed by its interruption.

"Ignore it," she said, obviously still startled by his pronouncement.

So was he.

He glanced at the screen on her phone.

Johnathan.

Fuck. "He doesn't give up, does he?" Sebastian asked.

Cheeks flushed, Ashley met his gaze. "I told him no," she said, more to herself than to him.

"No to what?" Sebastian was suddenly on alert.

Ashley sucked her bottom lip into her mouth before answering. "No to his proposal," she whispered.

He felt his eyes open wide, his heart squeeze inside

his chest until he found it hard to breathe. "Well, some guys need to be told twice. Idiots, obviously," he muttered, shaken by the fact that some other guy had proposed to the woman he was just getting to know again. The woman he wasn't ready to let go. "Sounds like you need to tell him no again, this time so he hears you loud and clear."

She narrowed her gaze at him. "What makes you the expert on relationships, anyway?" she asked, the phone having gone silent between them.

"Nothing. I've never had one, to be honest," Sebastian said.

"Exactly." She straightened her shoulders, sounding triumphant. As if she had him figured out, when, he realized, even he didn't understand himself at all.

He studied her pretty face. "You sound smug. Like you know all there is to know about relationships while I know nothing."

"Seems that way, doesn't it?" she asked.

He let out a low laugh. "Not in the least." But he wasn't surprised she couldn't see the truth for herself.

She crossed her legs, squeezing her thighs together, and glared at him, obviously waiting for him to explain, so he did.

"At least I know if I'm ever going to have a relationship, I'll have to figure it out for myself. Because my father sure as hell didn't set a good example. In fact, no woman's ever been worth the effort to even try, so I go from fuck buddy to fuck buddy."

"And you're proud of that fact?" She sounded horrified.

He shook his head. "But at least I know why I do what I do. Can you say the same? Your mother set a shitty example, too, but instead of going from guy to guy, you let one lucky bastard wine and dine you, never letting him get close. Seems to me the end result is the same." He folded his arms across his chest, certain he'd made his point. And in case he didn't, he added, "You might date nice guys but your walls are as high as mine."

"Stop the car." She banged on the plexiglass separating them from the driver.

The winder lowered. "Can I help you?" the driver asked.

"We're still in downtown San Francisco, right?" she asked.

"Yes, ma'am."

"Then stop the car. I want to get out."

"Ashley—" Sebastian reached for her, but the car came to a halt and she let herself out, as he scrambled to follow, grabbing her heels before exiting the car to go after her.

✦   ✦   ✦

ASHLEY NEEDED AIR. She wanted to take a walk and not discuss all the ways their parents had screwed up their lives and left them unable to form healthy relationships.

Sebastian caught up with her on the sidewalk, grasping her arm and easing her to a stop. "Hey. At least put your shoes on."

She hadn't even realized she was barefoot and she slipped her pumps onto her feet before meeting his gaze.

"I'm sorry. I didn't mean to upset you," he said.

She knew that. He'd been reacting to Jonathan's call right after he'd ... after they'd ... "Yeah. I know." She ran her tongue over her lips. "My mother loved my father," she said, needing him to understand. "I just don't remember those days. What I remember," she said slowly, "is her going from man to man in search of security. And I never want to be like her."

He brushed his knuckles over her cheek in gentle understanding. "So you found a man who didn't demand anything from you. Until he did. And then you broke up with him. Keeping your walls high. Like me."

She blew out a long breath and sighed. She just wished Jonathan would believe that over meant over. She hated the thought of what she'd have to return to in London, the conversation they were going to have to have again, face-to-face.

"Hey." Sebastian put a hand on her shoulder, and she tipped her head closer to him. "I know what it's like to learn truth about yourself that hurts," he said.

"I knew those things about myself," she muttered. "I just didn't appreciate having them thrown in my face."

He grinned. "Well, me neither. So join the club."

"Touché." She sighed. "I want to take a walk."

"Hang on." He strode over to the limo driver's open window and spoke to the man before returning to Ashley's side. "I asked him to wait for us," he said as he shrugged off his jacket and placed it over her shoulders.

She pulled the lapels closed, snuggling into the warmth of the fabric and the scent of him with a sigh.

"Ready?" he asked.

She nodded.

With his hand on her back, they started to stroll. They were, she realized, by Fisherman's Wharf, in Ghirardelli Square.

"Chocolate," she murmured, looking up at the ice cream & chocolate shop in the retail and dining area.

"I bet it beats Hershey's."

She laughed. "Why don't we find out."

They walked into the store, the scent of cocoa overwhelming her in the best possible way. And though she could have had one of the famous ice cream sundaes, she opted for her old standby, a chocolate bar.

It hurt her to admit, but the Ghirardelli was heaven in a chocolate bar. "Better than sex," she said, eyes closed, as the decadent chocolate melted in her mouth.

He met her gaze with a steamy one of his own. "Honey, you are definitely sleeping with the wrong men."

Chapter Six

SEBASTIAN KEPT ASHLEY by his side as they walked into the office for another day of digging into what the hell was going on at the Keystone project. He strode into the building and was greeted by the staff at the front entrance who checked in employees and approved entry. From there they headed upstairs.

Ashley had suggested they meet with Katherine Downing, head of Purchasing, in her office, where she would be more comfortable, and see what, if anything, she was keeping to herself.

Once there, they found the woman sitting at her desk. She appeared to be in her mid-thirties, with light brown hair cut short, and her desk was cluttered. Still, she worked diligently on the computer when they filled the doorway and didn't look up until Ashley knocked.

"Oh, hi!" She gathered the papers on her desk, straightening them into a pile. "How can I help you?" she asked, rising to her feet.

"Please, sit." Sebastian gestured with his hand, not wanting her to be uncomfortable or feel like they were at a formal inquisition. The woman lowered herself into her seat. "Mind if we join you?" he asked. There were two chairs across from her desk.

"Of course not."

When they were all in their seats, Sebastian leaned back, letting Ashley take the lead.

"We were hoping we could talk about the Keystone deal. I went through the receipts yesterday. I wanted to ask if there was anything you forgot to tell me about. Something you might have remembered last night?" she asked.

Katherine shifted in her seat, and Sebastian agreed with Ashley, she knew something she didn't want to say out loud.

"You seemed uncomfortable, yesterday and today." Ashley leaned in closer, her gaze drifting around the cluttered desk. "I see you have kids. They're adorable." She picked up the photograph of a little girl with pigtails. "She's cute."

The woman smiled. "That's Riley and this is my son, Brandon." Katherine pointed to another photo, this one of an older boy with a big grin.

"You need this job, yes?" Ashley dove into the meat of things. "And you're nervous about telling us something. You don't need to be. Your job is safe. We just need to know what's going on."

The other woman let out a deep breath and nodded slowly. "Okay, look. Mrs. Knight was in charge of the buying of supplies to get this office up and ready for the Keystone deal."

"Amanda Knight?" Sebastian asked and Katherine nodded. "Are you saying there were problems with her job performance?" he asked, an edge in his tone. One he hadn't meant but it was Ethan's wife they were discussing.

Ashley put a hand on his arm and squeezed tight, telling him silently to back off.

"Let's backtrack," Ashley said. "You said Mrs. Knight was in charge. Go on."

Katherine looked down at her hands. "Mrs. Knight picked the suppliers for everything we purchased. She told me who to buy from and I did it."

"That sounds pretty standard. The project manager makes executive decisions," Sebastian said.

Ashley elbowed him in the arm. "Did you find something wrong with the suppliers she chose?"

"Not exactly ... but..."

Ashley waited, and though it took all his patience, Sebastian kept quiet, too.

"She said she had connections that would help us later. For example, if we used the vendors she chose for the company cell phones, she promised they'd make us a good deal later, when we needed laptops. Except that good deal never materialized. And the phones, they didn't work well." The woman didn't meet their gaze as she gnawed on her lower lip. "But she was the boss's wife, so when she said to buy something, I did."

She glanced at them and handed Ashley a folder full of papers. "You can look through these," she said.

Sebastian met Ashley's gaze. "Thank you, Katherine. We understand. And don't worry about anything. Okay?"

Ashley rose from her seat and Sebastian followed her lead. They walked out of the room, and he led her to the office he'd appropriated as his own for the duration of his stay and shut the door.

"Amanda," he muttered with a shake of his head. "Katherine insinuated Ethan's wife did something wrong." His head swirled with the possibilities of issues they didn't yet know about. "She had a drug problem," he went on. "That meant she needed money, right?" He looked at Ashley, feeling tortured, mostly for Ethan.

Ashley's expression was as pained as his own. "We don't know anything yet," she said in an effort to reassure him and probably herself. "She just said that Mandy was in charge, something we already knew. We'll go through the paperwork again." She gestured to the folder she'd put on the desk.

He nodded, agreeing. But there was more. There was the insinuation that she'd chosen the wrong suppliers for a reason. He glanced at Ashley, feeling helpless.

"Hey. We don't know anything. There's nothing to go back to Ethan with ... yet." She placed a comforting hand on his arm, one that felt anything but platonic considering he'd had his fingers in her pussy just last night.

He bit back a groan. He couldn't think like that now, at work. He needed to focus on the problems at hand. "We can't discuss anything about Mandy with Ethan. Not until we know more."

Ashley nodded. "I agree. We'll get it figured out."

Sebastian's cell phone rang from his pocket. He pulled it out, and though he didn't recognize the number, because it had a San Francisco area code, he answered.

"Knight here."

"Mr. Knight? This is Corinne Fields, Stephan Romano's personal assistant. I know you've been trying to reach him. He'd like to extend an invitation for you to come to Sei Bellisimo, his vineyard in Napa Valley, and meet with him in person."

He raised an eyebrow in surprise. He hadn't realized the man was out of town.

"He'd like to send a car and you can spend the night at one of the guest cottages. He said you two have a lot to discuss."

Knowing the man was on the eccentric side and had known both his father and grandfather, doing this on his terms was important for keeping this deal in place while they figured out the lock issues.

"I'll be there. I have a ... business associate with me," he said, glancing at Ashley.

"No worries. We have multiple rooms in the cottage," she assured him. "I'll let Mr. Romano know you've agreed. He'd like to send a car for your trip to the valley."

"I have a limousine on retainer for my time here," Sebastian said.

"But Mr. Romano would much prefer to treat you to the trip."

Understanding again it was important to agree, Sebastian said, "Thank you. We can be ready to leave in a few hours." He gave the woman the name of the hotel from which to pick them up and disconnected the call.

He met Ashley's interested gaze. "I hope you like wine because we're going to Napa."

✧   ✧   ✧

ASHLEY HADN'T EXPECTED the trip to Napa Valley. Now, she stared out the window, taking in the green trees and the acres of rolling hills and vineyards along the way. Inside the limousine, she breathed in, smelling Sebastian's intoxicating scent and trying not to think about what had gone on the last time she'd been alone in the back of a limo with him for an extended length of time. But she found herself shifting in her seat anyway, sneaking glimpses of him when he wasn't looking.

He, too, stared out the window, deep in thought, she assumed about the problems with the business and the possibility of Mandy's culpability in some way. If she let herself think about it, the worry for Ethan when he found out would consume her.

Instead she focused on the fact that she was going out of town with Sebastian. True, she'd been sharing a suite with him without incident, unless you counted the limo, but this was a cottage in Napa Valley. There'd be wine. And conversation. And ... did she want sex?

Sure, she'd told him sex wasn't important, but that was before he'd kissed her until she couldn't think or feel anything but him. Last night she'd lain in the room next to his, thinking of nothing but sleeping with him. Of smelling the scent of his aftershave, her body revved up with desire, his big hands traveling over her breasts, tweaking her nipples, making her so wet that when he was ready, he'd glide into her, thick and pulsing.

"Jesus." She trembled at the thoughts going through her mind and pushed her hands against her thighs.

"Everything okay?" Sebastian turned her way, the scenery speeding by through the window behind him.

"Yes. I just didn't expect to take this trip," she hedged, not wanting to get personal with him just yet.

"I hope you don't mind. It's just another night in a different room. And maybe a tour of the vineyard and a drink or two of some of the best wine made." His easy grin made her smile.

"No, of course I don't mind. It actually sounds wonderful. I hope you get some good news from Stephan Romano about your contract with him."

Sebastian rolled his big shoulders. "I'm counting on the fact that he wouldn't send us his limo and bring us all the way up to his vineyard just to sandbag me."

"You're probably right." She liked his optimism.

"Besides, I appreciate the break. It gives me time to think about how to handle things when we return to the office tomorrow. What direction to go in when it comes to figuring out what's wrong and Amanda's role in it. I've gone over and over those papers Katherine gave us. It's something we'll deal with when we get back."

She nodded, reaching out and grasping his hand.

"We'll figure this out together."

"We're a team," he said.

She glanced down at their joined hands, his skin darker than her paler flesh. She pulled her bottom lip into her mouth and thought back.

What *did* she want from Sebastian?

Was sex on the table?

She knew if she gave him any indication she was willing, he would be, too. Her nipples tingled at the possibility of his mouth on them, his big hands gliding over her breasts. Yes, she wanted to sleep with him. She just had to quell the intellectual part of her brain sending warning signals that she couldn't get further involved with him and walk out unscathed emotionally.

But.

Sebastian didn't do relationships. He'd admitted as much. And she was going back to London when this situation was over and she knew Ethan was settled. So how much damage could a sexual relationship cause, especially when she was an expert at keeping her heart to herself?

She squirmed in her seat, knowing the decision was made. If the opportunity arose while they were alone in Napa, she was going to devour Sebastian like he was the tastiest chocolate bar she'd ever had.

✧   ✧   ✧

SEBASTIAN STEPPED OUT of the limousine and stretched his cramped legs. Ashley joined him, climbing out of the car and drawing her arms up over her head, her breasts lifting enticingly with the motion. He watched in fascination, the tips of her nipples showing through the fabric of her white dress. His mouth watered at the sight.

"It's warm out," she said, and he shook his head to clear it of any dirty thoughts threatening to take over after the long car ride, where he'd been achingly aware of her nearness with every breath he drew.

"It's hot," he agreed, sweating in his dark suit.

"Welcome!" A pretty brunette woman came rushing out from the nearest building to meet them, dressed in a tight black skirt and a silk blouse that hugged her curves. "I assume you're Sebastian Knight?"

He nodded. "And this is my ... associate, Ashley Easton."

"It's a pleasure to meet you," she said, her gaze fully on Sebastian. "I'm Corinne Fields. We spoke on the phone earlier."

She shook his hand, holding on longer than was appropriate for a business greeting, as she demurely fluttered her lashes.

He'd been this route before. She was interested. And in the past, he'd have reciprocated that interest for the time he was here. But for the first time, his attention was occupied with thoughts of another woman, rendering him uninterested in what this woman was offering.

Ashley was all he could think about. Being alone with her here. Seeing where things could go.

Ashley cleared her throat as he slid his hand out of Corinne's grip, aware of Ashley's gaze on the prolonged shake.

Not wanting either woman to get the wrong idea, he took a step closer to Ashley and away from Corinne.

Corinne stiffened, obviously getting the message. "Well, I'll send someone to take your bags to the cottage," she said stiffly. "It has three bedrooms, two bathrooms, and a fully stocked kitchen. You'll be very comfortable," she told them with a forced smile.

"Sounds wonderful," Ashley said, not engaging the other woman at all. "Can you tell me a little about the vineyard?"

"Sei Bellisimo means *you are beautiful* in Italian," Corinne said, explaining the name. "We're a boutique winery, a small, out-of-the-way vineyard, but even so, summer is a busy time in Napa and our tastings are all booked. However"—she turned to them with a professional smile—"we will be providing you with our very best wine at the cottage and during your private tour."

Sebastian nodded. "And we're very grateful, but my focus here is to meet with Stephan Romano." Although Sebastian had expected a tour, he'd hoped to do business first. "I'm sure you realize there's a lot on the line for our two companies."

Stephan Romano, however, was an eccentric, something he knew from his grandfather. Not only was he one of the biggest defense contractors in the world, he owned this vineyard, and he was reclusive and hard to get in touch with.

"Yes, of course. He has every intention of meeting with you," Corinne assured him vaguely.

Beside him, Ashley placed a hand on his shoulder, her first sign of personal interaction in front of Corinne. It was as if she'd read his thoughts and understood his frustration with the situation. Not only did he appreciate having her here, but her innate comprehension of what he was feeling and her ability to soothe him was something he wasn't used to.

"Would you like to change before I take you on a walking tour of the property?" Corinne asked.

In anticipation of a meeting with Stephan Romano, they had both remained in their work clothes.

Ashley glanced at Sebastian, and he inclined his head, leaving it up to her. He apparently wasn't going to be able to rush things.

"I'd love to change. I have sneakers in my suitcase," she said.

They were taken to their cottage and their bags were brought in. Ashley chose one of the rooms and disappeared into it. Sebastian had brought a pair of cargo shorts and a tee shirt, and it took him no time to switch clothes. Ashley emerged a few minutes later, wearing a cute pair of striped drawstring pants and a tank top, sneakers on her feet.

"Ready!" She bounced on the balls of her feet, obviously looking forward to the vineyard tour.

Corinne met them outside, and soon they were following her throughout the estate. As they walked along a crushed stone pathway, the crunch of their footsteps seemed loud in the utter silence surrounding them. It was hard to believe they were in Northern California and not some private villa, something out of another era. Mr. Romano had obviously had visions of his Tuscan ancestry when he'd built the estate. The fountains, marble statuary, and small wrought iron benches set in secluded, tree-and-vine shaded nooks practically invited one to laze away the day sipping the decadent wine they'd tasted that the vineyard was so famous for.

With Ashley by his side, as she was now, Sebastian thought. Their arms often brushed as they walked along the path, sending a sexual jolt through his system. Despite his frustration with Romano himself, Sebastian had enjoyed his time touring the winery with Ashley as they viewed the place where the 2016 Cabernet Sauvignon was created, along with their 2017 barrel-fermented Sauvignon Blanc. Corinne had obviously put the moment when they'd met behind her and so had Sebastian. Ashley didn't seem fazed, and they were all engaged in the tour.

Sebastian had even been impressed with the beautiful greenery lining the paths and the processes they saw. But every time he questioned when he'd meet with Romano, he felt as if he was being stonewalled.

Finally, Corinne took a phone call, listened, and said, "I understand. I'll let him know." She disconnected and turned to Sebastian. "Mr. Romano looks forward to having dinner with you tonight."

He nodded, relieved. "Good. Thank you."

Because as nice as this tour had been, the trip was about saving the contract and ultimately the reputation and financial stability of Knight Time Technology.

"I hate to leave you, but Mr. Romano needs me back at the office. It's a short walk back to your cabin," she said, gesturing in the direction Sebastian had already memorized.

"Thank you," Ashley said. "This was wonderful."

"Thank you," Sebastian said, as well.

Corinne smiled and excused herself, leaving them

alone on the path, surrounded by trees and the smell of fermenting grapes.

Ashley turned her face toward him, her cheeks pink from their time in the sun. "I know you want to get to the meeting, but I hope you enjoyed the tour."

"I did. I especially enjoyed the fact that you had such a good time." It had been a pleasure watching her take in the sights, sounds, and smells they'd experienced.

"The process was fascinating. And the wine was delicious." They'd sipped some during a brief tasting, not enough for either of them to get drunk.

He tapped her nose with his finger. "Freckles," he said, amused at how quickly her fair skin reacted to the sunlight.

Her irises darkened at his touch, and her pink tongue slicked over her bottom lip, a move that had his cock responding in kind.

Fuck.

He wanted her.

He didn't think he could spend another night in the room next to hers, imagining her naked between the sheets of her bed.

Their eyes met, gazes locked, awareness shifting between them. Her hair fell to one side, and he brushed the long strand back, using the excuse to touch her, his fingers gliding over the bare skin on her shoulder.

She trembled at the feather-light brush of sensation, her nipples tight buds beneath the stretch of her tank top. He ached to touch her, to taste her, certain one lick would exceed the richness of the wine he'd sipped here today.

"Sebastian." Her sexy tone told him she could read his mind, was in full agreement.

And when she rose onto her tiptoes, he met her halfway, his mouth coming down hard on hers. He swept inside and was lost in her sweet taste and the eager greeting of her tongue tangling with his.

He braced his hands around her waist and lifted her until she wrapped her legs around him, holding on tight. Her sex pressed willingly against his aching cock, desire ratcheting up inside him. She ran her fingers through his hair, pulling at the strands while holding him in place as he kissed her for all she was worth.

They'd been explosive as teens and were even more combustible now. He'd been with his fair share of women, and none had ever elicited this kind of desire in him. And dammit, it wasn't just the physical passion that burned so hot, it was the knowledge that she calmed something inside him when nothing and no one else ever could, that worked him into a frenzy for her, as well.

He slid a hand beneath her shirt, his palm gliding

over her back as she began to rub her breasts into his chest, her nipples hard points pressing against him and arousing him even more. The need to take things further hammered at him from the inside, his cock a hard brand in his pants.

He began to pull her shirt up higher, intending to take it over her head, when the sound of a bird screeching in the distance startled him, reminding him of where they were and the fact that someone could come upon them at any time.

"Shit," he muttered, lowering her to her feet and keeping her tucked against his chest. "Wrong place, wrong time."

She glanced up at him, a definite naughty gleam in her eye. "But there will definitely be a right place, right time later?"

He threaded his hand through her hair and met her gaze. "Count on it," he said in a gruff voice he barely recognized.

DINNERTIME FINALLY ARRIVED. Sebastian and Ashley had headed back to the cottage to shower – separately – an excruciating endeavor where his cock didn't want to understand why she wasn't in the steamy bathroom along with him. But once they'd returned to their cottage, they'd agreed on not having anything that might distract him from business before dinner with the company's biggest client.

That didn't mean, when Ashley stepped out of the room, wearing a fitted black dress and heels, he wasn't hard as stone and completely focused on how gorgeous she looked. Her hair was pulled back in a sexy updo with pieces falling around her face, which had gotten sunburned today. And her high heels drew his attention to her long legs and toned calves, making his mouth grow dry at the sight. She was his wet dream, had been since he was a kid.

And tonight he was going to find out what being inside her felt like. But the next few hours were all about business. "Ready to go, beautiful?"

Her cheeks flushed pink. "I am. You look pretty damned sexy yourself."

It took all his willpower not to drag her off to one of the bedrooms awaiting them.

They met Stephan Romano in a private dining room. He was an older man with a big personality who liked to talk about the old days, and he meandered in his storytelling. As much as Sebastian tried, Romano couldn't be pushed, swayed, or moved on in conversation until he was good and ready.

While they made small talk, they consumed the vineyard's Cabernet Sauvignon and a delicious rib-eye steak and potatoes au gratin and green beans. The man was alone, as his wife had passed away a few years ago, as he'd informed them, and he felt like he'd had the best. He wasn't about to go looking for someone who could never live up to replacing her.

A pang had settled in Sebastian's gut as the man had uttered those words, his body, mind, and soul aware of and consumed by the woman sitting at his side. For someone who'd never thought about a future, it was strange, the gnawing pain in his stomach as he considered Stephan's words. And how they might change his future if he let them. Then again, he was dealing with a woman who had a life – even another man – waiting for her in London, and who didn't believe in giving up her emotions to the opposite sex.

Whoa. He was getting ahead of himself, he thought. They hadn't even slept together yet. Just because she made him feel things ... new things, didn't mean he was ready to want more, either.

With that, his stomach settled, just in time for dessert, as a hefty piece of homemade Italian cheesecake had just been served.

As he refocused on Romano's ramblings, Sebastian realized the man had moved from discussing how his father had started the winery to how the American consumer's buying habits had changed and all businesses had to adapt along with them.

Somehow, despite his preoccupation with Ashley, Sebastian still felt his frustration grow because he desperately wanted to talk to Stephan about Knight Time Technology's contract with Keystone.

"Love the stories about your great-great-granddaddy helping Billy the Kid escape from jail," Stephan said. "Now there was a man who had his locks down pat."

His words captured both Sebastian and Ashley's attention.

She sat up in her seat, leaning in closer. Sebastian was completely ready to promise the man whatever he had to in order to appease him while they figured out their next steps.

"Now you know I've known your family for a long time, which is why I wanted to meet in person," Stephan said.

"And I appreciate that, Mr. Romano." Sebastian met the older man's brown-eyed stare.

"I told you, call me Stephan," he said in his booming voice. "I hate to say this, but we can't afford any more delays on the project."

"I know and I'm here to reassure you."

Stephan clasped his hands on the table in front of him, his gaze still on Sebastian. "This is our biggest headquarters ever, and we plan to open other facilities. Now, I wanted Knight Time Technology in on things, but when the most basic piece of security, the *locks*, aren't working properly..." He shook his head but didn't finish the sentence. He didn't need to. "I'm sorry, Sebastian. But I have to kill our contract due to nonperformance and bring in someone else to take over."

A wash of panic assaulted Sebastian at the man's words and definitive tone. This was his chance, his big opportunity to help his family, and goddammit, he was going to do it.

"Stephan, give me a week to find out what's going on and fix it." He managed to speak in a confident tone, understanding how badly they needed this extension.

"Now, son, I've given your company months, and we're no closer to solving the issue. What's so different now?" Stephan asked.

"Me. I'm the difference." Sebastian swallowed hard and did his best to exude complete faith in himself. "I'm out here now. I have a fresh, new perspective on things. Ethan's going over the prototypes again with our people–"

"Forgive me but hasn't Ethan been distracted because he lost his wife? I mean no disrespect–"

"None taken," Sebastian said. "We received your flowers and he appreciated the gesture. But I promise you, he's on top of things on his end, and I'm here in person to handle mine."

He felt Ashley's gaze on him, watching him, felt the pressure to succeed. "One week," he said, hearing the slight edge to his voice and wishing he could make it disappear.

Beneath the table, Ashley's hand slipped onto his leg, her palm wrapping around his thigh. She meant it as another sign of reassurance, he knew, but his body reacted immediately, his cock swelling thanks to the nearness of her hand. But he gritted his teeth, and as she loosened her grip but kept her hand on him, he found himself calming down. Her touch grounded him.

Stephan drummed his fingers thoughtfully on the table. "Well—"

"As you said, our families go way back," Sebastian said, willing to grab on to anything to gain an edge. "So for the sake of family…"

Because the man frowned, his next words took Sebastian by surprise. "One week," he agreed.

"Thank you. You won't be sorry," he assured the older man.

Now he just had to fulfill his promise.

They headed back to the cottage a short while later in silence, Ashley obviously sensing his need to think. Once back, Ashley excused herself to change, and he poured himself a glass of red wine, leaving one for her as he settled on the front porch in a comfortable outdoor chair.

He sat, drinking a delicious glass of red wine, his cell phone on the table in front of him. Ethan had called a few times during the day and again this evening, and Sebastian had ignored him, not wanting to tell his brother he had no news. He certainly didn't want to let Ethan in on the fact that Stephan Romano wanted to cancel their contract and bring in another company to take over.

Production was still working on the existing issue, and Sebastian was trying to find out where the money had gone that should have been available to buy new materials. Although he should feel relieved about the extension, and he did, he was also on edge, knowing how much of the family's future sat on his shoulders. A week wasn't much time given what they needed to do. He wanted to buy himself another day before he filled Ethan in.

He took a sip of wine and stared up at the night sky, stars dotting the inky blackness above. He'd wanted the chance to prove himself to Ashley and to his brothers, and now he had it. A definite case of be careful what you wish for, he thought, swirling the liquid around in the glass.

"Hi." Ashley's voice broke into his thoughts.

He glanced up to find her walking toward him

wearing a short light blue robe, belted loosely around her waist, giving him a luscious view of her cleavage and her long legs as she drew closer.

He placed his glass down on the table beside him and extended a hand. She slid her palm against his, and he pulled her onto his lap, the scent and the heat of her arousing his already stimulated senses.

He'd been waiting for her for what felt like longer than just the past half hour, and she was finally going to be his.

Chapter Seven

"I STILL CAN'T believe what happened with Stephan," Sebastian said to Ashley, finding that her presence took away the edge of anxiety that had been riding him since dinner. "He really intended to pull the contract from Knight Time Technology and he'd have had every right."

She met his gaze, hers steady and sure. "But you handled it really well. You were self-assured and confident. You gave him what he needed to see, and he has no idea how fragile the situation really is." She placed her arms on his shoulders. "You've got this," she said in a reassuring tone.

Her faith in him after everything they'd been through was humbling and much needed.

He grasped her hand. "*We've* got this. Starting to-morrow, we need to dig deeper."

She nodded. "But tonight—"

"Tonight is for us." He needed her and he intend-ed to have her.

She tipped her head and started in for a kiss, but

before she could press her lips against his, he stood with her in his arms and headed inside. He kicked the door shut behind him and made his way to his bedroom, lowering her to her feet, her body gliding along the hard length of his cock that was thick with desire.

"Sebastian." She reached down and cupped him through his slacks, her palm pressing against his erection, and he groaned.

He grasped her wrist and brought it up over her head. "You don't want things to end too soon."

A seductive smile pulled at her lips. "Of course I don't, but you wouldn't deny me a feel would you?"

He leaned in and slid his lips over her neck, grazing her with his teeth.

"Trying to distract me?" she asked, her body trembling. "Because it's working." She hooked a foot around his ankle and used the anchor to rock her pelvis against his, her softness in all the right places brushing along his hardness.

"Dammit," he muttered. This woman was sugar and spice, tempting him with all the facets of her personality, and now she was teasing him. Testing his restraint.

It was time he took over this seduction. He grasped her shoulders, turned her around, and reached for the tie on the robe, undoing the silk and slowly lowering the garment down her shoulders, revealing creamy white skin.

Leaning in, he pressed his lips to her bared flesh, feeling the way her body trembled at the feather-light touch. He slid the sides over her arms and let it fall to the floor, leaving her clad in a sexy pair of black lace panties and a matching bra that he could only see from behind. The indentation of her waist enticed him; the soft curve of her ass had his palms itching to cup, his mouth watering to taste.

He wrapped an arm around her waist and pulled her against him, letting his cock wedge into her rear. He trailed his lips over her shoulder, letting his palm splay against her stomach, his fingertips dipping low into the elastic of her panties.

She sucked in a breath, trembling against him while he rocked himself against her and slipped his fingers lower, trailing over her sex. "Do you have any idea how hot you make me?" he asked.

"I can feel how hard you are," she said, wriggling her hips so his cock ground against her ass.

She was damp against his fingers, wet for him as he played with her lips. "I want to feel you, hot and wet around my cock," he told her.

"I want that, too." She turned in his arms and faced him.

Reaching behind her, she released the bra clasp and let it drop. Looking at her gorgeous round breasts, dusky nipples, hard and peaked, had him holding on by a bare thread.

As she reached for her underwear, hooking her thumbs into the sides and pulling the pair down over her hips, he was done. Ready.

He unbuttoned his shirt in record time, and her hands shook as she helped him unbutton his slacks. He pulled off his pants and underwear at the same time, finally naked along with her.

She splayed her hands over him and he let her explore, gritting his teeth as she kissed his neck, petted his chest, and paused to just breathe him in. "You smell so good," she whispered against his skin.

He dipped his head and inhaled deeply. "You smell better." A heady mix of vanilla and feminine arousal, he thought, wondering if he'd ever taken his time to savor any woman before.

He could breathe her in forever.

He was hard as stone, but they'd waited a long time for this moment and he wasn't going to rush it. But apparently she had other plans, because before he could decide whether to lay her down on the bed and devour her or kiss her senseless right here, she took him off guard, dropping to her knees before him.

She slid her hands up his thighs, teasing him, until she grasped the hard length of him in her hand and slid her mouth over the head of his cock. He groaned, his hand coming to rest on the top of her head.

He hadn't seen tonight going this way, had planned to have *his* mouth on her pussy, his tongue between her sex and on her clit. But he couldn't stop her, not now that she'd licked him all the way down and slid her tongue back up again, swirling her lips around him like a giant lollipop hers for the taking.

He gathered her hair into his hand and held on as she sucked him deep, hollowing her cheeks as she pulled him in. God, he didn't think he'd ever seen anything as sexy as this woman on her knees before him. In and out, sucking his dick, pulling him to the back of her throat and releasing him again.

His legs shook and stars spun behind his eyes as she brought him to the brink of climax. He grasped harder on her hair, holding on as he suddenly came, his entire body consumed by the friction of her mouth, the intense pleasure overwhelming him.

It took a lot for him to get himself together. He pulled her to her feet, pushed her onto the bed, came down over her, and kissed her hard. He thrust his tongue into her eager mouth, tasting himself on her as he devoured her in the only way he could at the moment. Because she'd milked him dry, though he couldn't deny his cock was already getting hard at the thought of being buried deep inside her.

Her hands came up to cup his face, and her kiss

softened, so his did as well, until they'd broken apart, breathing heavily. He looked into those desire-filled eyes and knew he was ready to go again. He'd thrown condoms in the nightstand drawer in the hopes they'd end up here.

"Show me," she whispered.

"What?" he asked.

"Why sex is better than chocolate."

Before she could say another word, he crashed his mouth against hers.

ASHLEY'S BODY WAS burning with desire. Sebastian lit a flame inside her no man ever had before. Somehow an act that she'd merely tolerated before had become one she'd needed to do for him. She'd had to taste him, to bring him pleasure when she'd only done the obligatory blow job before. She knew she wasn't particularly good at it, but it hadn't seemed to matter. He'd come fast and hard, and his big body had shaken and trembled. Thanks to her.

Now he kissed her hard, his mouth bruising her with the intensity of his lips on hers. But the kiss didn't last long. He lifted his head and trailed his mouth over her throat, down her collarbone, and over her breast, pausing at her nipple. He tugged one into his mouth, sucking on her until she felt the pull straight down to her clit. He nipped and laved and bit again until she moaned out loud, which had him switching breasts just in time because she was so damned sensitive there, she didn't think she could handle any more.

His big hands trailed over her belly, sliding down to her sex. He slid his fingers through her slick folds, his touch an electric wire through her body, arousal cascading through her. So this was what good sex was like. And he hadn't even been inside her yet.

She was used to men who performed fast and got out quickly. Sometimes she wasn't even aroused enough. To her, sex was part of a relationship but no big deal. But *this* was what she remembered from when she'd kissed Sebastian as a teen. The overwhelming desire. Her pulse pounding hard, her rapid heartbeat.

The need for this one man.

And then his fingers were gliding over her clit. Sliding into her, finding a spot inside her that had her soaring. She came fast and hard, her body suspended with pleasure, as he touched her and played her until the waves subsided.

Then he reached for the nightstand, tore open a condom, covering himself before coming back over her. He looked into her eyes and her heart twisted inside her chest. She ignored it, choosing to focus instead on the pleasure that awaited her, although she couldn't imagine how she could feel anything better than what he'd done so far.

Until he slid into her, his thick arousal parting her and filling her up completely. His eyes had locked on hers, and he didn't break contact, the connection between them a tangible thing.

"Sebastian." She curled her hands around his shoulders, digging her nails into his skin. "You feel so good."

"So do you. And I'm going to make you feel even better." He pulled out and thrust back into her.

She was overwhelmed by the sensations he created in her body, the feelings he evoked inside her. Bracing his arms on either side of her head, he raised his body and began to glide into her, over and over.

She gasped at the delicious invasion, every thick inch of him bringing her higher and higher, closer to climax. He raised himself off her and slid his hand between them, gliding his fingers over her sex, spreading her juices as he began to rub circles over her clit.

Her hips bucked at the sensual assault on her senses, everything inside her attuned to his touch, and with one more swipe, she shattered, waves of pleasure suffusing her body.

She moaned and shook through her release, and as she came, he let go of his restraint, taking her hard, his body pounding into hers. It didn't take long for him to climax, too, his release triggering another wave inside her that had her coming along with him.

He collapsed on top of her, his breath warm against her neck, his body heavy on hers. She was awed and overwhelmed, completely taken off guard by the intimacy of the act between them.

She'd asked him to show her great sex. Instead he'd shaken her up inside, too. She'd felt things she wasn't used to feeling, and it frightened her.

He rolled off her, rose to a sitting position, and walked to the bathroom. She used the time to pull herself up in bed and gather the covers around her, just as he strode out of the bathroom, totally confident in his nakedness.

"You gonna let me in?" he asked, pulling at the covers and sliding in beside her. "Are you okay?" He sounded concerned as he gathered her close.

"A little thrown off, to be honest."

"Was it that good?" he asked, in an obvious attempt to lighten her mood.

She nudged him with her elbow. "Yes. It was that good." She settled into him, telling herself there was no reason to panic.

She'd had great sex with a man who had already told her he didn't do relationships. She wasn't ready for one, anyway, and the end of her time here meant she'd be going back to London. It was all fine.

She exhaled a long breath and eased down on the pillow.

Sebastian pulled her into him and wrapped his large body around hers. "Relax," he said, brushing her hair and putting his head into the crook of her neck. "And go to sleep."

She decided there was nothing to be gained by worrying and listened to him, drifting off with surprising ease.

She woke up to the most delicious sensations sparking between her thighs. Sebastian was licking her sex, waking her up in the most arousing, delightful way.

She moaned, rolling over and spreading her legs so he could settle himself more comfortably. She glanced down, his dark head in stark contrast to her fairer skin, as his head bobbed in time to the motions of his tongue. He licked and tortured her with long laps and quick darts against her clit, finally pushing up inside her.

She gasped at the sweet invasion, twisting and rolling her hips as he ate at her, waves of pleasure building inside her. Her hands came down to grasp at his hair, pulling at the silken strands as he devoured her.

Her orgasm built fast and furiously inside her, and when he slid his tongue over her clit and pulled, she came apart, shaking and trembling for a long while after the tremors subsided.

He wiped his lips on her thighs, then climbed up and over her. "Good morning," he said in a gruff voice.

"It is now. Hell of a way to start the day."

"I agree. Especially because we have a long drive back to look forward to."

She reached for him but he shook his head. "We need to get going. I just figured that was a better wakeup than an alarm clock." He pulled off the covers, baring her naked body. "Come on. Let's shower." His eyes darkened as his gaze slid over hers. "Fuck the time. Shower sex sounds like a better idea," he muttered, picking her up and carrying her into the bathroom.

SEBASTIAN HAD FELT the tension in Ashley's body after they'd made love last night, and he saw it in her eyes any time she let herself think too much. He had chosen those words going through his mind deliberately. Making love. Because if there was one thing Sebastian knew, it was what they'd experienced last night went way beyond sex.

He sure as hell had plenty of experience with the latter, and what they'd shared? That had been something special. And though to his surprise, he was ready for more, with Ashley, she was not. He'd have to lead her there slowly. Become part of her life and engage her emotions so by the time she was supposed to be ready to leave for London, she wouldn't want to go.

Wouldn't want to leave him.

But he left her to her thoughts on the trip back to San Francisco, understanding he shouldn't push too hard. For now, he'd focus on the situation with the business. It would keep her by his side.

And that's exactly where she belonged.

✧　✧　✧

THE FOLLOWING MORNING, over coffee, Sebastian dove into the papers Katherine Downing had given them the other day. In his mind, he had a dual purpose to his investigation of what was going wrong with the Keystone contract and the locks they'd supplied. One, of course, was to fix the problem and keep the contract alive. The other was to find out what, if anything, Mandy had done wrong during her time in charge of this project.

Ethan kept his problems very much to himself, and if his marriage had been in trouble, Sebastian hadn't known.

He'd already received a text from Ethan, informing him that the developers didn't believe the software was the issue with the locks. That left the hardware.

He studied the purchasing paperwork, noticing one company coming up over and over again. It wasn't a familiar name.

"Good morning." Ashley smiled, joining him on the terrace.

She wore a yellow sleeveless dress and bone heels, looking sexy and put together and ready for a day at the office. A far cry from the woman he'd had screaming his name last night.

He hadn't had to cajole her to stay in his bed, either. For all that she might be emotionally skittish, she must have come to some deal with herself that let her join him in his bedroom.

He could live with that. For now.

"Morning." He gestured for her to take the seat next to him. "Coffee?" he asked and she nodded.

He poured her a cup and she added her cream and sweetener. She took a sip, closing her eyes and sighing as the caffeine hit her system. The sound went straight to his cock.

But this morning he was focused on business.

"Find anything interesting in the paperwork?" she asked, taking another long sip before reaching for a yogurt that had been served along with muffins by room service this morning.

"Yes. This company is mentioned a lot. Plenty of

purchases from Sparrow Electronics."

"Is that odd? To buy a lot from one company?" she asked, peeling off the top of the yogurt and dipping her spoon inside.

He shook his head. "No, but I've never heard of them, which doesn't mean anything. Still..." He picked up his phone off the table and dialed his brother. "Parker," he said when his sibling picked up the phone.

"How's it going?" his brother asked.

"No results yet. But I have a company I need you to look into. Sparrow Electronics. I need the name of the guy Mandy dealt with there. And I need to know their products are top-notch."

"Sure thing. Are you onto something with a defective part?"

Sebastian ran a hand through his hair. "I don't know anything yet, but when I do, you'll be the first to hear." Because together they'd figure out what to say to Ethan if there was an issue with anything his deceased wife had done.

"I'll look into it and get back to you with a name and information."

"I'm going to talk to the head of Purchasing again today, so I might have the name soon, too." He was beginning to think Katherine had wanted him to find the answers on his own without her having to snitch to him with information. She'd handed over the papers too eagerly.

"What aren't you telling me?" Parker asked.

He wasn't willing to share the burden until he knew something for certain. "Gotta go, Parker. Talk to you soon," he said, disconnecting the call.

He glanced at Ashley and she treated him to a reassuring smile. "Thank you," he said, surprised when the words left his mouth.

"For what?"

"For being my rock."

She glanced up at him in surprise, her eyes softening as she met his gaze. "If I can give you that, I'm glad."

"You do." He left it at that. "I'm going to have to meet with Katherine Downing again. I think she's holding out on me." He placed a hand on the file of bills.

"She has children. She needs the job."

He nodded, having already thought about that. "I'm going to have to push her."

"Do what you have to do," Ashley said. "You have no choice."

He treated her to a grim smile. He took in her empty yogurt cup and finished coffee. "Ready to go to the office?"

She nodded. "Let me grab my purse."

Time to find out what the hell was really going on at Knight Time Technology in California.

ON THEIR WAY to the office, Parker called back. Ashley couldn't help but hear and realized it hadn't taken him long to find out that Sparrow was a new company that had opened up seemingly overnight. They didn't have a track record with big companies buying from them, and Sebastian told her that made him nervous.

Once at the office, Ashley followed Sebastian into the conference room where Katherine Downing waited for them. Ashley had asked him if he wanted to deal with the woman one on one, but he'd insisted she join him.

His rock.

She didn't know what to make of that statement, but she was glad she could be here for him when he needed her.

Katherine had chosen a seat on the longer end of the conference table, leaving the head for Sebastian. He took it, settling in.

"Katherine, how are you?" he asked, clasping his hands on the table.

"Good. Good." But her forehead beaded with per-spiration, her nerves at meeting the boss again, this time in a private conference room, showing.

"I'm going to be honest with you," Sebastian said. "Your job is on the line. Anyone having anything to do with this project isn't safe if Knight Time loses this Keystone contract, so I need honest answers. Do we understand each other?"

She nodded solemnly, bobbing her head quickly.

Ashley knew this hard line wasn't easy for him, but she also understood what was at stake. She was proud of him and how he was handling things. From Ethan, she knew Sebastian hadn't taken his personal life seriously, though he'd tried to stand up for the business in the past. But she could see the changes in him now, as he found his footing and worked to save the company. He was a man she was coming to admire, something she never would have thought possible upon her return to New York.

"Good. Now, you gave me the purchase orders for the project and I went through them," Sebastian said. "Let's start with Sparrow Electronics. I noticed we bought most of our components for the locks from them. In fact, we purchased the main component from them. As the head of purchasing, you signed off."

"Yes, sir."

"I need to see all the bids."

She flushed red. "I–"

He pinned her with a harsh glare.

"They aren't the lowest bidder," she said, the words tumbling out as she twisted her hands together on the table.

Ashley glanced at Sebastian, whose gaze had narrowed. "Why the hell not?" he asked.

She wondered that as well.

"Umm—" Katherine clearly didn't want to answer.

"You picked a high bid from a new, untried company, and I want to know why," Sebastian pushed.

"It wasn't me," she said. "I mean, it wasn't my choice." Tears formed in her eyes. "Please, Mr. Knight. I have kids. I'm a single mom and I need this job."

"Just explain it to me," Sebastian said, his voice gentling. "I'm not here to be the bad guy. I just need to get to the bottom of things."

The other woman swallowed hard. "Okay. It was Mrs. Knight who made the final decisions on which bids to take."

"Mrs. Knight?" Ashley asked. "Amanda Knight?" Her stomach churned at the direction this conversation was taking, and though it wasn't her place to jump in, she couldn't help but ask.

"Yes," Katherine said. "She told me what to order and from which company. I questioned her. It didn't make sense to me why we were paying so much more for components than we had in the past, but she said it wasn't my place to question things." Katherine glanced down. "I'm sorry. I didn't want to say anything about the boss's wife. Like I said, I really need my job—"

"It's okay," Sebastian said, his voice gruff. "I asked you for the truth and you're giving it to me."

Ashley knew this news wasn't any easier on him.

"Do you have the name of the person Mrs. Knight dealt with at Sparrow?" Sebastian asked.

Katherine nodded. "Jasper Nichols."

Sebastian blew out a long breath. "Thank you, Katherine. You can go back to work now."

She stood up, obviously shaken.

Sebastian rose, too. "Your job is safe, Katherine. You did as you were told. It's fine."

Her eyes lit up in relief. "Thank you, Mr. Knight. Thank you." The other woman rushed out of the room, leaving Ashley and Sebastian alone.

He glanced at her, concern in his eyes.

"What are you thinking?" she asked him.

"That we need to find out more."

She nodded in agreement. She glanced down at her hands, realized she was twisting them together just as Katherine had been. "Right. Just because Mandy paid more for components than the company had in the past doesn't mean the parts are bad, right?" she asked, holding on to hope.

"Right. But—" Sebastian frowned, causing her

stomach to flip in renewed concern. "The fact that this Sparrow Electronics doesn't have a legitimate business record isn't a good sign."

She swallowed hard. "Then we keep digging."

He nodded. "I need to talk to Greg Munson, our head engineer. Find out if any of the Sparrow components could be causing an issue. The damn problem is so intermittent, it's been hard to narrow down. And we need to track down this Jasper Nichols and find out what his business relationship was with Mandy."

"All before we tell Ethan, right?" she asked.

"Right. I don't want to hand my brother another blow when he's just begun to grieve."

Ashley's heart softened at Sebastian's love for his sibling. The fact that he didn't want to hurt Ethan without one hundred percent proof spoke volumes about the man Sebastian was deep inside.

A man Ashley was very afraid she was falling for.

Chapter Eight

A FTER MAKING AN endless number of phone calls to Sparrow Electronics to speak with Jasper Nichols, only to be told he was out of the office, and having the man not return his messages, Sebastian called Parker once more. This time he asked his brother to look into the man himself. They pulled in Sierra, as she was the social media guru and they needed to find a way to locate the man, swearing her to secrecy about mentioning anything to Ethan.

In the meantime, it was time he saw the campus where the failing locks had been installed. They'd only put them in on one building, having discovered the flaw in the design immediately on installation.

He called Corinne Fields and asked her to get him permission to enter the Keystone campus. A little while later, he and Ashley had shown their IDs at security and signed a non-disclosure agreement that had been left waiting for them, and their car pulled up in front of the main building.

They left the driver out front and headed inside. A

security guard met them at the door and showed them to an office where a tall man with military bearing met them.

"Mr. Knight? Ms. Easton? I've been expecting you." The man shook each of their hands.

"I spoke to Mr. Romano and he said to let you walk around the building. We're not up and running yet, so you can see what you need to and check in with me again before you leave. Every office room has a lock," he informed them.

"Thank you."

Sebastian placed his hand on Ashley's back and led her out of the room.

"Tell me about the smart locks your company is doing for Keystone," she said as they took the elevator up to the fifth floor, where Sebastian had been told the first locks were installed.

He glanced around. The entire building had been wired to provide what the occupant needed without being asked. Smart heating and cooling, occupancy sensors that acknowledged when people were in various parts of the building and turned on accordingly, and emergency notification systems that communicated with both the main Keystone office and local police and fire departments. Among other things.

Including the smart locks.

"Let's see. Smart locks are designed to lock and unlock a door upon receiving instructions from an authorized device using wireless protocol and what's known as a cryptographic key to execute authorization process."

She laughed at his technical explanation. "I'm almost sorry I asked."

"It's a little confusing," he acknowledged with a wry grin.

"But, in essence, you need a lock and key to work, except the key isn't a physical one but a smartphone or special key fob configured to wirelessly perform the process."

"I understand. Sort of. It's wireless communication."

"Correct, but there is also hardware involved, as you saw from the purchase orders."

She nodded in comprehension as they walked to the open room they saw there. "Like these." She placed her hand on the metal casing on the door.

"Exactly. I wish I could look at them and know what was wrong." He frowned in frustration and walked over to the window overlooking the corporate park.

Ashley strode up behind him and wrapped her arms around his waist, looking out over his shoulder in silence. "We can't do anything here. Why don't we go back to the hotel?" she suggested.

He liked the idea. Being here only reminded him of what wasn't getting done.

ASHLEY NEEDED TO get Sebastian out of his funk. They drove back to the hotel in silence and took the elevator up to the suite, where he pulled off his tie and kicked off his shoes, easing back in a chair. But she sensed the frustration rolling over him in waves.

She toed off her heels and walked over to where he was sitting. "You need to relax."

"Yeah? You have any ideas how?" he asked, his mind obviously totally on business.

"How about ... this?" She slid her hair over one shoulder before turning around, giving him her back. "Unzip my dress?" She glanced at him and batted her eyelashes.

His eyes darkened at her obvious intent. "You're trying to distract me."

She grinned. "Is it working?"

He glanced down at the bulge in his pants, his thick erection pushing against the fabric of his pants. "What do you think?"

She backed closer to him. "Unzip."

He eased the zipper down her dress, parting the fabric and pressing a kiss against her bare skin. At the warm touch of his lips, her nipples puckered into hard peaks, desire pulsing down to her sex.

She shimmied out of the dress, letting it fall to the floor, then hooked her thumbs into the edging of her panties and pulled them off.

His gaze was hot on hers as she moved to undo her bra and let it drop on top of her other clothes. With a low growl, he undressed, too, undoing his button-down and revealing his sexy abs and flat stomach. A dark sprinkling of hair trailed into the waistband of his pants, which he began to undo.

Rising, he dropped his trousers, pulling his boxer briefs down with them. She watched, fascinated, as his thick erection sprang free, a drop of pre-come on the head.

She licked her lips at the sight and he groaned. "Not this time. This time I'm taking control."

She sensed he needed that, and her sex got wet at the thought. So instead of sliding onto his lap the way she wanted to, so she could feel all that hardness against her, she waited to see what he'd do next.

He rose and hooked his arm around her waist, leading her to the edge of the sofa. From behind, he wrapped his hands around her body and cupped her breasts, kneading them with his palms. She moaned, tilting her head against his shoulder, reveling in the sensations he evoked inside her. He pulled on her nipples and her pussy spasmed, desire slamming into her. She choked back a cry, but he apparently heard her and tweaked harder on the tight buds.

Her legs trembled and she needed more than he was giving her so far. And damn him, he knew it, but he obviously wanted to torment her. His erection sat in the crack of her ass as he spent a good long time plucking and playing with her breasts, his mouth nibbling at her shoulder and neck all the while until she was begging for more.

"Sebastian, please." She pushed her ass back into his waiting cock, which was hard and thick against her.

He braced his hand on her back and pushed her down so she was bent over the arm of the sofa. She drew a breath, ripe with anticipation, knowing she was soaked between her thighs and she wanted him badly.

He stepped away from her, and then she heard the crinkle of a condom, and soon he stepped back behind her, the thick head of his erection pressing between her legs and nudging at the opening of her sex. He kept a hand on her as he glided his thickness into her, and she groaned with a combination of relief and renewed desire.

His hand slid from her back to her hair, holding on tight as he began to thrust into her from behind.

"Oh God," she groaned as he filled her up.

He drew back and she had but a second to miss his

thickness before he took her hard again. He hit a spot inside her that had her seeing stars, pushing her closer to an explosive orgasm with every renewed thrust.

The tug on her hair was a surprising arousing addition to the sensations taking over her body. And though she ought to feel distant from him, what with the way she couldn't see his expression and he controlled their every movement, she'd never felt closer to a man. Knowing she trusted him to give her pleasure, not to hurt her but to send her soaring, lent a shocking intimacy to the act. Not to mention the innate understanding she had that he needed to be in control in this instance, when the rest of his life was out of his hands, and that she could give him this bonded them in some crazy way.

He curved his free hand around her waist and slid his fingertips over her clit.

She cried out, arching her hips to take him deeper, and then she lost track of where his hands were and how he was touching her. She only knew he was taking her hard, hitting all the right spots. Sending her spiraling into a climax that had her screaming.

His harsh groan followed soon after, and he thrust once, twice, and a third time before she felt him pulsing inside her.

"Jesus," he muttered as he pulled out of her.

"Yeah."

"Bed?"

She nodded, needing to get off her feet. He helped her stand before pulling off the condom and tying it off. He headed to the bathroom and she made her way to the bedroom. He caught up with her, hooking an arm around her waist and tossing her onto the bed, coming down beside her.

✦   ✦   ✦

SEBASTIAN PUSHED HIMSELF back, pulled Ashley against him, settling them side by side against the pillows on the back of the bed.

"Are you okay?" he asked, because he'd taken her hard, bending her over the sofa and pulling at her hair. Not looking into those beautiful eyes.

He winced at his behavior, but her cheeks were glowing, despite the fact that she wasn't meeting his gaze.

"I'm good. Really good. I wanted you to take what you needed," she said. "And I'm glad that you did."

God, she was amazing. Pulling him in deeper every day they were together, every night she spent in his arms. He didn't know what kind of progress he was making with her emotionally, probably wouldn't know until it was time for her to leave him. His stomach twisted at the notion, and he pushed the thought aside. They had a lot to do between now and then.

He turned his attention to them now instead. He was fucking starving. At that moment, her stomach growled and he chuckled. "That answers my next question. You're obviously hungry, too. Do you want to order from room service or Grub Hub?" he asked of the food delivery service.

They ended up debating, then ordering hamburgers from the hotel and chocolate cheesecake for dessert.

"You're going to make me fat," she said to him, curling into his arms, where she felt oh so perfect.

He frowned at her comment. "That has never been an issue except in your mother's warped mind." She'd always been perfect to him.

"I think I'm brainwashed sometimes," she mused.

He knew she was talking about her mother. "What do you mean?" He smoothed her hair down so it wasn't in his face, but she rolled over so she could face him.

"Mom used to make me watch what I ate so I would attract men."

He coughed out loud. "As if that was ever an issue." He'd had plenty of friends interested in the girl who'd moved into his house. Only Sebastian's threat to bloody a nose or three kept them from making a move.

"Well, for Mom, she wanted to be some man's

trophy wife, be it your father or the next sucker." She winced. "God, I didn't mean to call your dad a sucker."

He couldn't help the grin that hit his lips. "If the shoe fits… Every woman he's had since my mom has been his version of the perfect country club woman."

She nodded. "And my mother has wanted to be kept." She wrinkled her nose in disgust. "And it's not that I want to be thin for any particular reason, it's that I hear her voice in my head. *Healthy eating makes for a healthy body, Ashley. And then the right man will take notice.* She just didn't mean healthy in any correct way. But old habits die hard."

He groaned. "We sure do come from dysfunction," he said. "Do you keep in touch with your mother?" They hadn't discussed her relationship with her only parent before now.

She swallowed visibly and hard. "On the holidays and birthdays, if she remembers mine, because otherwise I call her. Mostly because she's my mother and it's the right thing to do. I have to be able to live with myself, after all."

He could see the pain in her eyes at the admission, one he understood more than she knew. "Same here with my dad. I'll check in because he's my father. But I know he's the reason for a lot of my past bad behavior. Whether it was punishing him or following his behavior by example without even realizing it. But those days are over."

"Why?" She tilted her head and met his gaze. "What changed for you?"

He hesitated, gathering his thoughts, debating how much to tell her. She didn't need to know how many women he'd been with, how often. "A few things hit at once, to be honest."

"Mandy's death."

He nodded. "My family couldn't reach me the night she died." He recalled the pain he'd felt on hearing the news, the desperate need to get to his brother. But he'd also sensed they didn't know how badly he'd felt. How much he'd hurt for Ethan.

He refused to tell Ashley where he'd been that night. "But when I heard, I rushed right over. That morning, I found out about Mandy's drug problem – and that Sierra and Parker had already known. They hadn't trusted me enough to tell me."

"Oh, Sebastian." Ashley cupped his chin. "Some people grow up at different speeds than others, but your family should have included you."

He rolled his shoulders, leaning his head against the headboard. "I don't know. I understand now they had their reasons. And when you told me what you'd overheard the night in my father's study, I went home and really thought about not just who I was – but who

I wanted to be."

It'd hurt, too.

But she listened in silent understanding and also, he sensed, support, something he couldn't say he'd ever had in quite this way before. She wasn't judging him and that meant everything.

"I saw a guy who thought he took life seriously but who really wasn't focused on business or family the way he should have been. I saw," he said, drawing a deep breath, "a guy well on his way to becoming too much like his father."

He looked into her soft gaze and didn't see pity. Instead he caught both understanding and what he wanted to think was caring.

"It matters," she said.

"What does?"

"The fact that you've been introspective. That you want to change and are." She treated him to a warm smile, just as a knock sounded at the door.

She glanced at him with wide, panicked eyes because they were both stark naked. He grinned.

She dove toward the bathroom, giving him a nice view of her ass as she ran.

"One minute," he called out toward the door. Then he grabbed a pair of jeans from the closet and slid them on before walking to the door and letting the waiter in with their food.

They ate and he felt like a weight had been lifted from his shoulders. Sharing with her who he'd been, who he'd feared he was becoming and acknowledging his attempt to change had lightened some of the burden he'd been carrying – because he knew he was making those changes.

He only hoped they were enough to win the woman in the end.

✦   ✦   ✦

FIRST THING THE next morning, Sebastian's phone rang, startling him because he'd been in a deep sleep. Ashley lay wrapped around him, her head in the crook of his arm, her knee across his legs, her sweet pussy pressing against his thigh.

Annoyed because the phone had beat the alarm, he answered without looking at who it was. "This better be important," he said gruffly into the phone.

"It is." Parker's voice sounded over the line. "Worth waking you."

"What time is it?" Sebastian asked.

"Five a.m. your time."

"Who is it?" Ashley asked, still sounding half-asleep.

"Is that Ashley? Are you two sleeping together?" Parker asked, sounding surprised.

She buried her face in his chest, and he could only

151

imagine how red her cheeks now were.

He slid a comforting hand over her bare back. "It's none of your fucking business, Switzerland. What's going on?"

"Sierra and I did the digging you wanted on Jasper Nichols. I can't believe what she found."

Completely awake now, Sebastian pushed himself back up against the pillows. Ashley pulled the covers up over herself and leaned in so she could hear the conversation, as well.

"Jasper Nichols hasn't been in business long, that much we know, which begs the question, why did Mandy do business with them? Not to mention, he spends most weeknights at a club called Marquee. Sierra looked into the place and it's great if you want to score drugs," Parker said, sounding disgusted.

"Shit," Sebastian muttered.

"There's more," Parker said.

Sebastian glanced at Ashley. "Go on."

"Check your phone. I'm sending you a picture Sierra found on Nichols' Instagram account from about four months ago."

"Hang on." Sebastian lowered the phone from his ear, switched apps, and waited for the picture to load.

It took a while but eventually a photograph came up. A guy with shoulder-length brown hair sat in a dark nightclub with a very familiar woman on his lap.

Bright red lipstick stained her normally pale, glossed lips. Her eyes were heavily made up and she wore a slinky black dress that showed off ample cleavage. But despite the overly done makeup and barely there dress, there was no mistaking the woman whose face stared directly at the camera with glazed eyes and her arms around the man's neck. His fingers, meanwhile, dipped below the cleavage of her top.

"Mandy," Ashley said, sounding horrified.

"Right," Parker said, this time not commenting on Ashley's presence in Sebastian's bed. "And the guy in the picture is Jasper Nichols."

There was no doubt there was more going on between Nichols and Ethan's wife than purchasing orders.

"Dammit." Sebastian's hand curled into a fist.

Ashley grasped his hand and smoothed out his fingers in an attempt to relax him. "Ethan doesn't know, does he?" she asked, obviously past caring that Parker knew they were together.

"Hell no. I figured we have to decide what the hell to do," Parker said. "So I called you."

Sebastian didn't miss the fact that Parker had turned to him for a solution. He ran a hand over his hair and groaned. "We get the full story of what went on here, and then we bring it to Ethan, no speculation involved."

Ashley's eyes gleamed with approval.

"Agreed," Parker said. "Sierra doesn't want to hurt him, either. So we're all sworn to silence until you two figure out their relationship. Any ideas how to do that?"

"We'll head over to that club tonight and have a talk with *Mr. Nichols,*" he said with no respect in his use of the man's name. "I'll get back to you when I know more. Hopefully this is a lead on what is wrong with the locks, too. I'm going to meet with Greg Munson this morning. Discuss the Sparrow components with him. I should know more then."

"Thanks, Sebastian. You're doing great out there," Parker said, taking him by surprise.

His heart warmed at his brother's praise. "Thanks, man. I'll be in touch." He disconnected the call and met Ashley's gaze, her expression disturbed.

"This is awful," she said.

He couldn't deny the obvious. "Listen, I want to take you to buy a dress for tonight's trip to Marquee. Something you don't normally wear, that won't look out of place. We don't want to stand out. I want Nichols to talk to me, not run the other way."

"You want me to buy a sexy dress?" she asked in a husky voice, running her fingers through his hair as she spoke.

His entire body responded to her teasing touch, his

cock now tenting the white covers. "One that's going to make every guy in the place look twice. At which point I'm going to have to kick the ass of anyone who glances at you sideways," he muttered, suddenly not liking his plan all that much.

"I'll need a pair of fuck-me heels," she murmured. "The kind that'll let me swivel my hips and make you drool."

He curled his hands into the covers. "As long as I'm the one who gets to bring you home and fuck you in them later, I'll live with it," he said.

She lowered her head, brushing her lips back and forth over his before lifting her head. "I don't want to think about Mandy cheating on Ethan." Pain flashed in her eyes.

"Me neither." Not until they had to. "So let's do something to make us forget." He pushed the sheets down to his legs and kicked them the rest of the way off. "C'mere," he said in a gruff voice.

She pushed herself up and straddled his lap with her naked body. His erection stood proudly between them, just waiting for her to act.

She slid her fingers over the droplets of come on the tip and his cock twitched at her sensitive touch.

"Condoms?" she asked.

He reached over to the nightstand where he'd stashed some and handed her a packet. Eyes gleaming, she tore open the foil and pulled out the latex covering, placing it over him and rolling it down his shaft.

"Ready?" he asked.

A seductive smile pulled at her lips as she rose and positioned herself over him, teasing him by gliding down oh so slowly.

"Oh God," she said and, without waiting, released her tight hold and took him inside her completely.

"Fuck." He gritted his teeth at the amazing feeling of being clasped in her wet heat.

And then she began to move, a seductress, gliding herself up and down on his shaft, as she rode him, head thrown back, her moans uninhibited.

He grasped her hips and held on as she took her pleasure. He didn't know how he held on as she built higher. She was gorgeous, cheeks flushed, breasts bouncing, the sounds of ecstasy filling his ears.

And then her tone changed, her eyes closed, and she let out a shuddering moan that undid him, sending him spiraling into his own climax. They came at the same time, his entire being lost to the woman holding not just his cock inside her body but his heart in her hands.

Chapter Nine

ASHLEY DIDN'T BELIEVE in cheating, which was why she was so upset about Mandy and Ethan. Love might not be something she understood, but commitment was. And Mandy had violated the most basic of understandings between two people. Even Ashley, for all her faults when it came to deep relationships, would never cheat on someone she cared about. And she certainly wouldn't want someone doing it to her.

She glanced down at her hand, firmly clasped in Sebastian's bigger one, and her heart flipped over. If another woman laid a hand on him, her claws would definitely come out, she thought. She understood that much about their relationship.

A few minutes later, as they walked into Knight Time Technology, her phone rang, and seeing Jonathan's name sent her reeling.

"Who is it?" Sebastian asked as they walked through the lobby.

"A friend from home," she said. Which wasn't a

lie. She just didn't want to get into an argument with him over nothing. "I'm going to take it down here. Why don't you go meet with Greg Munson." They'd agreed the man would be more comfortable talking to Sebastian alone anyway.

"Sure." He shot her a glance but kissed her lips and headed inside anyway.

She answered the cell, stepping toward an empty bench by a glass window overlooking the parking lot. "Hello?"

"Ashley, finally. I've been trying to reach you."

And she'd been ignoring his calls. "Jonathan, I told you, I have a lot going on here … and we're over. I don't think we should be talking on the phone."

She wasn't a fan of men and women being friends after they broke up. She knew some of her girlfriends enjoyed keeping in touch with their exes, but she wasn't one of them.

"That's why I'm calling," he said in his formal British accent. "Because I think, being in the States, you're forgetting what we shared. And I wanted to remind you of the good times."

She sighed and glanced out at the palm trees lining the parking lanes. "We did have good times," she agreed with him. "But I explained to you, I don't love you and you deserve that from someone. Goodbye, Jonathan," she said before he could continue to try and talk her around to his way of thinking.

Her heart beat harder in her chest. She hated hurting him, but she'd been honest. Kindly honest, until he kept calling. She disliked having to explain her feelings over and over again. And the more he pushed, the harder it was going to be when she got home to London.

Having taken a call from her boss earlier in the day, she knew her time off was running out. At that thought, nausea filled her, which she attributed to the upsetting phone call. Clearly Jonathan had talked himself into believing they had something they could build a lifetime on, but she just didn't feel that way about him.

She didn't get flutters in her stomach when she thought about him, and never had. She didn't have feelings of longing when they were apart. Nor did she look forward to seeing him in a way that had her insides flipping with excitement and joy. All things she felt when she thought about Sebastian.

She cared more for him than she had for Jonathan. More than she did for any man in her past. She liked waking up with him in the morning, knowing his face was the first thing she saw when she opened her eyes. He always made sure she ate lunch and dinner and he'd bought a stack of chocolate bars when they were at Ghirardelli and snuck one in her purse every day.

There was something special about Sebastian Knight, and she would be a fool not to recognize that or the fact that she was falling for him.

He was showing her what a real relationship was all about, digging his way into her heart, slowly but surely. She was feeling things that were new to her, and she was afraid that what should have been a simple affair was becoming far more emotionally complicated, when she'd always kept things with men casual and easy.

But she also knew her entire life was in London. The flat she rented and had turned into her refuge, the plants her neighbor was watering for her, and the job she really did enjoy. One she'd had since graduating university. She couldn't deny that the satisfaction she found working with Sebastian to save the Keystone contract was greater than any work-related success she'd had back home ... but London was just that. *Home.*

And when this project with Sebastian was over and she knew Ethan was settled, she was headed back there.

For good.

Ignoring the pain in her stomach at the thought, she headed for the elevator to go meet up with Sebastian and get back to work.

✧   ✧   ✧

ASHLEY WAS MORE subdued after her phone call, but she said she was fine, and he didn't want to push her to open up if she didn't want to. Instead, after finishing his meeting with Munson, where the engineer examined the bids and receipts from Sparrow Electronics and promised to look into those specific parts, he guided her back to the limousine.

He helped her into the back, then walked around to talk to the driver, where he found out his best bet for women's dresses was the Filmore Street shops, and he instructed the man to take them to that shopping district.

He joined Ashley in the back of the limo, closing the door behind him.

"Where are we going?" she asked.

"Shopping, like I said earlier." He slid a hand behind her back and pulled her close. "We're going to dress you up for the evening on the company dime."

She glanced up at him with wide eyes and a big smile. "You know what? I'm going to let myself enjoy it," she said, surprising him by not arguing with him over money. He was glad. He wanted to treat her and let her have some fun.

The car pulled to a stop in front of what looked like a boutique, with short women's dresses in the window, sequins shimmering as the sun hit the glass.

The driver opened the door and let them out, and

Sebastian escorted her up a few brick steps and into the store.

A saleswoman caught sight of them as they entered and rushed over to greet them. "Good afternoon! Can I help you with anything?" she asked, her gaze going from Sebastian to Ashley.

"She needs a dress," he said.

"For going to a nightclub," Ashley explained.

The woman nodded. "Which one? That way I can guide you to something appropriate."

"It's called Marquee. A friend of mine recommended I check it out while I'm in town," Ashley said smoothly.

The saleswoman smiled. "Then you want something chic and fun." She tipped her head to the right. "Come. I know just what I want to show you."

A few minutes later, Sebastian was waiting outside the fitting room while Ashley changed inside. The saleswoman went to answer the phone. Sebastian glanced at the time on his phone. He knew women took a while to change, but he couldn't help but think this was excessive.

He walked over to the open doorway leading to the dressing room. "Ashley?" He called.

"Yes?"

"Are you coming out any time soon?" he asked.

"No," came her reply.

They'd been in the store long enough for him to know nobody else was back there with her, so he strode through the doorway and toward the one room with the closed curtain.

"Ash? Let me see."

She peeked her head out. "I'm naked."

He chuckled. "I've seen you naked, so that's not an issue. Come out and show me."

"You've seen me naked. The rest of San Francisco hasn't."

He laughed harder but now he was really curious. "Let's see."

"Fine."

She stepped out from behind the curtain in a beaded silver dress that barely covered her private parts. Her cleavage exploded from the center of her chest, deep cutouts ran along the sides, revealing her flat stomach, and the hem was extremely high on her thigh.

His body tightened at the sight of her curves in that sexy dress, but that wasn't the reaction she was looking for at the moment.

He cleared his throat, and before he could speak, she turned around, revealing the line between her thighs and buttocks and a definite hint of cheek. No way was he giving any other men that glimpse of her ass.

"I am not going to a club like this," she muttered, at the same time he said, "You are not going out in that excuse for a dress."

She spun around, a pleased grin on her face. "Well, since we agree…"

"We'll find another store." He wasn't exposing her body for the sake of finding out anything about Mandy and who she was or wasn't sleeping with or buying shitty electronic parts from.

The saleswoman was disappointed and wanted to show them another dress, and Ashley gave in, letting her bring in a different type of garment. Half an hour later, they left the store with a short, flirty, according to Ashley, dress that covered her breasts and ass.

Later that night, every man in the nightclub still turned and looked at Ashley as she entered. In high silver heels with red-soled bottoms and a matching silver dress that dipped low in the front but left enough to the imagination and a hem that ended high on her thigh, her hair in spiral curls down her shoulders and back, her lips a teasing red pout, she was a guy's wet dream.

But she was his dream and he wasn't leaving her side in that sleazy club. Because the saleswoman had been on target with her initial dress choice and even at his most inebriated, Sebastian wouldn't have touched any woman here.

What the fuck had been going on with Mandy?

Drugs, he thought sadly. She'd been addicted. Had Jasper Nichols helped supply her?

He held on to Ashley's hand as they wound their way to the bar area, all the while scanning the place for the man they were looking for.

"White wine?" he asked her.

She nodded.

He ordered himself a scotch on the rocks and her Sauvignon Blanc, wanting to hold a glass in his hand. He'd been going light on alcohol since his self-revelations and didn't intend to change that now.

Sebastian tipped the bartender, then leaned in and asked if the man knew Jasper Nichols.

He pointed toward the back corner of the bar, a dark area that Sebastian hadn't focused on before. "He's back there with his crew."

He glanced at Ashley, suddenly wondering if he should have left her home.

"Come on," she said eagerly. "Let's go meet the man."

She obviously didn't have any qualms about who they were dealing with.

Drawing a deep breath, he pulled her behind him, keeping her close as he started toward the small crowd of people congregating together.

He reached the group and cleared his throat.

"You want something?" a beefy-looking man asked.

"I'm looking for Jasper Nichols."

"Who wants to know?" the man asked, folding his arms across his chest.

"He was friends with someone I know. She told me to look him up when I got to town."

"What's the friend's name?" the man grunted at him.

Ashley stood beside him, letting him handle things.

"Amanda Knight," he said. "Mandy to her friends."

Awareness swept across the man's expression and he pushed through the crowd, the parting of people revealing Jasper Nichols, who sat at a table, white powder in front of him. With his long, shaggy hair and lean face, he looked exactly like his photograph.

The bigger man whispered something in his ear, and he looked Sebastian and Ashley's way.

Nichols rose from his seat. Unlike Sebastian, who wore a pair of black pants and a button-down black shirt, Jasper Nichols dressed in a pair of jeans, a tee shirt, and a shiny jacket. His hair was slicked back off his face. "I heard you're a friend of Mandy's," he said, glancing at Sebastian.

"You could say that," he said.

His gaze then raked over Ashley, his eyes taking in

166

her body, darkening at the sight. "You a friend of Mandy's, too?" He licked his lips and Sebastian drew a steadying breath.

"Yes," she murmured.

"Well, you're as fucking hot as she is."

Pissed now, Sebastian wrapped an arm around Ashley's waist and pulled her against him. *She's with me, asshole*, he thought to himself.

Getting the hint, Nichols raised his hands, as if to say, *I didn't mean any harm*. "Where's Mandy been?" he asked, changing the subject. "She said she was going to New York and she'd be back. Instead she's gone radio silent." Nichols met Sebastian's gaze.

"Mandy died," Sebastian said bluntly, and beside him, Ashley leaned into him, offering support.

"Come on." The other man nudged Sebastian's free side with his elbow. "That's a bad joke, man."

"No joke. She OD'd," he said, remaining deadly serious.

Nichols' eyes opened wide. "No shit." He took in Sebastian's intent expression. "What do you want from *me*?" he asked, finally realizing Sebastian wasn't here to shoot the breeze.

"I want information. I want to know why Mandy was doing business with a company as new as yours. And why she paid you way above market price for parts we could have gotten at a more reasonable rate from better-known places." And that was just for starters, Sebastian thought.

"Whoa. All I know was Mandy asked me to get her cheap parts and I did." The man's face flushed red.

He'd done a hell of a lot more than that and he knew it. "Did she ask you to write up bids for higher prices, too? So we'd pay more for piece-of-shit components?" Sebastian asked, curling a hand into a fist.

Ashley grabbed on to his arm but he shook her off.

"What did you two do with the extra money?" he asked, continuing to push for answers.

Nichols looked panicked, as if he wanted to run, so Sebastian grabbed him by the collar. "Talk," he said. "Or I'm calling the cops and they can deal with the cocaine on the table behind me," he said into the other man's ear.

"The bitch wasn't worth it," Nichols muttered. "She wasn't even that good of a lay. Fine. We split the profit," he spat.

"Did you split the blow, too?" Sebastian asked in disgust before releasing the man.

Nichols fixed his shirt, smoothing his hands down his chest and straightening the collar. "She promised me more business after this contract. Then she disappeared. Now I find out the bitch is dead. Fucking waste of time."

Before Sebastian could take a swing at him, Ashley wrapped herself around him, locking his arms in place. "We got our answers. Now we're going home," she said, meeting his gaze in an obvious attempt to calm him down.

He nodded and let her lead him out of the club, knowing there would have been nothing good that could come of him taking a swing at the bastard. Mandy had made her decisions and ruined her marriage. Unfortunately he was the one who had to break the truth to his brother.

ASHLEY LET THEM into the suite and shut the door behind them. Sebastian hadn't said a word since they left the club, and she gave him the space he needed, obviously understanding he was processing all they'd learned.

"Can I get you a drink?" she asked, walking into the dimly lit joint area.

He shook his head. "No. Thanks." He strode over to the window and looked out into the dark night.

"Sebastian, you need to talk to me."

He spun around to face her. "What the hell am I going to tell my brother?" He said the first thing that was on his mind. "That on top of being an addict, on top of her being responsible for stealing from the company, his wife cheated on him?" He heard the rawness in his voice, and it matched the pain in his chest.

Ashley placed a hand on his chest. "I'll be beside you if you want. So you don't have to tell him alone."

Although he didn't know who needed to be present when he spoke to his brother just yet, her offer to be there meant everything. "Thank you. I'm just still trying to come to terms with it all."

She nodded in understanding. "Let's break it down. What will you do about the business? How will you get the parts fixed?"

He drew a deep breath. Business. This he could focus on easily. "We'll have to confirm the issue with the engineers, then funnel money from Peter to pay Paul, so to speak. Ethan will deal with the accountants and figure out how much we need for new parts and get it done. At least we've now narrowed down what the issue is."

"But you have to tell Ethan about how the company got into this position to begin with. About Mandy."

"Right." Which brought him back to the part he didn't know how to deal with or fix. He couldn't make this better for his brother and that killed him. "I'll call Parker in the morning. He'll talk to Sierra. I know that we need to do it in person, that's for sure."

She took his hand and led him to the sofa. He lowered himself onto a cushion, and she joined him, curling a leg beneath her. The short dress pulled way up her thigh, revealing a hint of her barely there panties, and he swallowed a groan. Not even a serious conversation could distract him from wanting her.

She met his gaze. "It won't be easy but you can handle it," she said, her mind still on their conversation. "And Ethan's strong. He'll be okay ... eventually," she said, as if she were certain.

And she probably was, because she knew his brother so well. "I need to ask you something," he said.

She tipped her head to the side. "Go ahead."

"Tell me about you and Ethan." Not because he was jealous, per se, but because ... yeah. He was jealous. Of the time Ethan had had with her over the years when Sebastian had had his head up his ass.

He wanted to understand their bond.

She sighed. "It's just going to make you feel bad and that's not what I want."

"You already told me he made sure your birthdays weren't forgotten and you mentioned Christmas." He'd gotten over that punch in the gut. He knew they had a sibling-like relationship, and he could handle that.

She nodded. "Okay, well, Ethan couldn't always

come to London. He had your family to be with, too. But he sent gifts on the holidays. He tried not to miss a birthday in person." She looked up at him through fringed lashes. "And he came to my graduations. Not even my mother did that. And though my education was on your father's dime, I know that was because she worked it into the divorce agreement, that he paid for me so she wouldn't have to give me a thought."

"I'm sorry," he said.

"No. We're past those kinds of feelings and regrets."

"We are," he agreed. "I just wanted to understand who Ethan is to you."

"Well, we talked on the phone in between visits and I got to know him really well," she said. "Mandy, too, for a while. But he was and is like a brother to me."

"So you knew about Mandy's problems. He confided in you." He swallowed the hurt of the knowledge that Ethan hadn't thought he could trust Sebastian that way.

"Yes, I knew. And I knew how, when she returned from San Francisco, she was distant. They did have their issues."

"I didn't know. Ethan didn't confide in me that way." He met her understanding expression. "I regret the way I acted all those years. The careless running around with women, thinking I knew all there was to know about my family and the business, all arrogant and self-assured, when I knew nothing at all."

She grasped his hand and held on tight, giving him strength. "Your brother loves you. Ethan always understood that we all grow up at different times. He's going to be proud of what you did out here. He'll see how you've changed, just as I do."

He'd needed this conversation with her, to understand his brother, but also, he realized now, to understand more about himself.

She had insight even he hadn't had.

But he knew now that he and his siblings would get beyond the past, he promised himself. Because he was more self-aware now. And he'd make a concerted effort to be a more present part of his brothers' and sister's lives.

"You see the good in me?" he asked, because they really did have their history, and now? They had great sex but he felt so much more.

"I do." She crawled onto his lap, hiking her dress up on either side of her thighs and taking her place on top of him. "The more I've gotten to know you, the more I do see the good in you, Sebastian Knight." Bracing her hands on either side of his face, she leaned in and pressed her lips against his.

He groaned and slid his tongue into her mouth,

and she wrapped her arms around his neck, holding on tight as he kissed her back.

This was everything he desired in life, everything he needed. And as she shimmied out of her underwear and helped him undress, all he could think about was getting inside her, where he belonged.

She threaded her fingers into his and rose above him. "Condom," she said, pausing and torturing them both.

"Pants pocket," he said through clenched teeth.

A few seconds later, he was good to go.

Her hands on his shoulders, she slid down onto his shaft. He felt every inch of his cock enclosed in her wet heat. She clenched tight around him, and he let out a rumbling groan of pleasure.

Her soft moan followed as she began to rock her hips, pivoting back and forth with her pelvis, her pubic bone and clit rubbing against him over and over again.

In all his years of cynicism when it came to women, he'd never have imagined he'd have found the answer to life deep inside one he'd known all along.

Because he loved her. A bone-deep, all-consuming love, he realized, as she came apart above him, taking him along for the ride. And as he came back to himself, her body still tight around his, he wondered how the hell he could manage to keep her.

Chapter Ten

ARLY THE NEXT morning, Sebastian met with Greg Munson, who had spent the night with his team, and they all agreed, it was a Sparrow Electronics purchase of a small component that had thrown off the locks and caused the problem. They hadn't caught it themselves because the prototypes had worked fine and the problem at Keystone had been intermittent.

The replacement and new install would cost a small fortune, but it was their only option. Sebastian called Parker, they pulled Ethan into a conference call, and without getting into the hows and whys, explained what the issue was and what they needed to fix it. Ethan agreed they had no choice but to fund a new purchase of the components from a reputable company and get a team in to reinstall at Keystone. They also agreed to hire someone to oversee the San Francisco office full time instead of sending someone out, as they'd done with Mandy.

Putting off Ethan's questions hadn't been easy, but Parker had agreed the conversation about Mandy had to happen in person. They were first and foremost a family, and this would be handled in an intimate manner, not over the phone like it was just another business mishap.

Sebastian's next call was to Stephan Romano, who, after reassurance that they'd discovered the problem and a promise to have the locks up and working in a reasonable amount of time, agreed to keep the contract in place.

Sebastian could finally breathe easy, knowing he'd accomplished his primary goal on this trip. He'd kept the Keystone contract secure. Later that morning, he called a meeting of the heads of all departments together and admitted that although things at Knight Time Technology had gotten off track, the days of lack of oversight were over. Or rather, Mandy's oversight, but nobody said as much out loud.

He knew he was leaving their San Francisco office in better shape than he'd found it, and he was pleased with that.

They took a late flight back to New York. Sebastian was preoccupied with what they would be facing when they returned.

Ethan's pain.

Ashley's eventual leaving.

And he wasn't sure how to handle either.

✧　✧　✧

176

ASHLEY WAS RELIEVED they arrived back in New York too late for her to talk to Ethan. She didn't want to be the one to break news to him that was best coming from family. No matter how close they were, he needed to hear about Mandy from his brothers.

She'd spent the quietness of the flight thinking about her relationship with Sebastian, wondering how she'd let herself get into a situation where she was going to be hurt when she left him behind. What in the world had she been thinking?

The truth was, for the time she'd been in California, she hadn't been thinking at all. She'd been feeling. Operating on sexual desire and emotional need. From the time she'd met him, Sebastian had understood her. Filled a need no one else ever had. And now, as adults, they'd come together like two pieces of a puzzle that had taken a long time to fit.

But now they were back in the real world and she had to think forward. Think smart.

Sebastian walked her to her door, pulling her luggage in one hand, his in the other. She let them in and he deposited her bag inside her room before meeting up with her again in the living room.

"Any chance you'll come up after you unpack?" He treated her to his sexiest, most charming smile.

The one that made her weak in the knees and soaked her panties. But it wasn't just sex she wanted from him, it was the emotional security he provided her, the knowledge that they made a good team, were a strong pair, that had her shaking her head and saying no to his question.

Though she and Sebastian had been sharing a suite in California, the fact was, they lived in separate apartments in New York. No matter what she felt for him, London, her job, and her life awaited her. The sooner they got used to being apart the better.

"I'm tired," she said. "I didn't rest much on the flight, and we have to be up early tomorrow to meet with Ethan."

His grin turned into a frown. "Why do I get the feeling you're pulling away?"

She rubbed her hands over her arms and turned away, not wanting to face him. It was one thing to pull back, another to look him in the eye while doing it. Not when all she really wanted to do was throw herself into his arms. But she lived in reality. So here they were.

"Hey." He grasped her and turned her around. "I have a question for you."

"Okay…" she said warily.

"Why are you still here?"

"What?" She hadn't anticipated that question.

"Why are you still here, in New York? You said you came for Ethan, but when he sent you away, you came with me. And now we've wrapped things up. We're talking to Ethan in the morning. Is your flight home booked?" As he spoke, his hands on her forearms felt like a brand, a reminder that she belonged here, with him.

And she couldn't let that sway her. Although she'd put work out of her mind, she had checked in with her bosses while she was away, assured them she was returning. She'd bought herself another week, that was it. They understood her leave of absence but wanted her back as soon as possible.

"I'll take your silence to be a no," Sebastian said, releasing her arms. "Which brings me back to why? Do you still want to be here? Or are you avoiding Mr. Perfectly Nice?"

She didn't want to talk about any of this. She still had a week left, and in that time, Ethan would need her once he found out about Mandy's cheating. Or was that just an excuse? Because she wasn't ready to leave Sebastian, her conscience asked her.

She glared at him. "Why are you pushing me so hard just because I said I was tired?" she asked, more annoyed with herself but taking it out on him.

"Because of what we shared in California. Because of what we feel for each other, even if you're not ready to admit it. And because I want to know."

Without warning, he pulled her in and pressed his

lips to hers. She let him in immediately, her body responding to his without thought or concern. It was only her mind that was driving her crazy. Her tongue glided against his, everything inside her flowering open for him. She curled her fingers into the material of his shirt, beginning to pull his tee shirt out of the waistband of his jeans.

And then suddenly she was standing alone. He'd pushed her away and met her gaze. "I want you to admit that you came here for Ethan but you're still here now for me."

"It doesn't matter why," she said, her lips still tingling from the force of his kiss. "I'm not here for good and we both know that. I'm leaving in a week," she whispered. "And it's better that we start to separate from each other now." Before she got even more attached to him than she already was.

"If that's what you need to tell yourself in order to sleep at night, go right ahead. I'm not going to deny there's something strong between us," he said, his voice softening. "I refuse to ruin a good time between us with an argument. If you want to sleep, sleep."

Leaning in, he brushed his lips over hers and walked out the door, leaving her with more to think about than she was ready to deal with at the moment.

❖   ❖   ❖

SEBASTIAN LET HIMSELF into his apartment and slammed the door behind him, the scene with Ashley tormenting him, making him wonder and second-guess himself. He hadn't said *I love you* because Ashley hadn't been ready to hear it. Instead the words still ran around in his head, begging to come out. But he knew mere sentiment wouldn't change her mind about returning to London. He didn't know what would.

He barely slept that night and dragged himself into the office the next morning, coming in early to talk to Parker and Sierra, to make sure they were all on the same page. Ashley was there, as well, once again dressed for the office in New York, wearing a fitted lavender dress and off-white heels, her hair pulled back in a bun.

Her walls were firmly in place.

He had every intention of burning them the fuck down.

One week. That was all the time he had to win the girl. The girl who'd used the entirety of the flight from San Francisco to pull away from him and last night to patch any holes in her defenses.

Well, look out, he thought. He wasn't letting her go without a fight. But right now he had important family business to take care of, and his brother and sister had walked into the room.

After he hugged both of his siblings, they talked

about what Sebastian had already told Parker of the situation with Mandy.

"I think you should be the one to tell him, Sebastian." Parker studied him, his gaze intense. "You went to California and got the news firsthand. He'll respect the fact that you came to him directly."

Sebastian's stomach twisted at the thought, but at the same time, he acknowledged that his brother was handing him the reins. Trusting him with something huge to the family.

Sierra nodded in agreement with Parker. "But we'll all be there to help him pick up the pieces."

"Ashley?" he asked, looking to her for confirmation and agreement with his siblings. After all, she knew Ethan as well, if not better, than they did.

"I agree. He should hear it from someone he trusts, and in this case, the best person is you." Her eyes met his, her gaze softening as she spoke.

She understood why he was asking her, knew he wanted her support in this. And despite their conflict at the moment, she was there for him, the way he'd known she would be.

A few minutes later, the family had gathered in Ethan's office. Big brother sat behind his desk, wearing a dark gray suit and tie, his expression serious. He was still mourning, Sebastian thought. Mourning the wife he thought he knew, and Sebastian was about to blow his world apart.

"Welcome back," he said, glancing at Ashley, then Sebastian. "I understand you had a productive trip." He sounded pleased with them.

Sebastian nodded. "Now that we know what's not working and why, new components will be ordered today. Romano's calmer. He's giving us breathing time. But you need to know what happened and why. How we ended up in this position in the first place."

"I assume it had something to do with Mandy." Ethan picked up a round paperweight from his desk and passed it back and forth between his hands.

He glanced not at his siblings but at Ashley. She gave him a subtle nod and it helped. "Ethan," he began, then decided to give it to him straight. "Mandy was buying inferior products from an unknown distributor at an inflated price. She and the head of the company were pocketing the difference."

A muscle ticked in Ethan's jaw. "Go on."

"And she was having an affair with him." Sebastian forced the words past the lump in his throat. "The bastard told me himself." Sebastian didn't mention that they had a photo from the man's social media. There was no good in showing Ethan his wife on another man's lap.

Ethan's gaze hardened. "Thank you for not sugar-coating the truth," he said. "You can all go now."

"Ethan, I know this is a shock," Sierra said, as Ashley came up behind him and put a hand on his shoulder.

"It is what it is. I appreciate hearing it and I don't want a pity party. So do me a favor, everyone. And go."

Sierra glanced from Parker to Sebastian, obviously at a loss. She strode over to Ethan, kissed his cheek, and walked out. Parker slapped him on the shoulder and did the same. Sebastian took his cue from his middle sibling.

He walked up to Ethan. "I'm here for you," he said, then turned and left the room, leaving Ethan alone with Ashley.

ASHLEY STOOD IN Ethan's office after his siblings had gone and bit down on the inside of her cheek, wondering if she should leave or force Ethan to talk to her. His family had left, so maybe they knew better. Turning, she started for the door.

"Wait," Ethan said.

She looked back and paused.

"I'm going to be fine," he told her.

She couldn't help the small smile that pulled at her lips. "I know that. You're strong."

"I also already knew."

She narrowed her gaze on his. "Knew what?"

He placed the paperweight he'd still been holding down on his desk. "I knew that Mandy was cheating on me. The marriage had been shit for a long time, and she was stretching out her time in San Francisco. She didn't even try to hide the late-night phone calls, when she'd slip out onto the terrace." He rolled his shoulders, the burden of what he'd been carrying big and painful. Hurt washed across his expression. "Things were a mess for her and between us. And I couldn't fix it."

And Ashley knew how much he'd wanted to. That was Ethan's MO. He liked to make things better for the people he loved. And at one time, he had loved his wife.

"I'm sorry," she said for lack of anything wiser or better to add. She spread out her hands. "You deserved better."

He blew out a long breath. "It hurt," he admitted. "Still does."

She walked over and took his hand. "I don't have anything to offer but clichés. Like, it'll get better with time."

He let out a low chuckle. "I didn't know she was stealing from the business, but I knew something wasn't right. I needed you and Sebastian to figure out the details. Thank you for going with him."

She nodded. "It's all settled now."

"And you're going back to London soon?" he asked.

"Next week." She swallowed the lump in her throat at the thought of leaving. "Unless you need me longer? I can talk to my bosses—"

He shook his head. "You've done plenty. Thank you." He studied her for a long while, until she was squirming beneath his stare.

"What?" she asked.

He braced a hand on the desk and said, "He's going to miss you, you know."

At his stark, unexpected words, she blinked in surprise.

"Sebastian," he continued before she could play dumb, because she didn't want to talk about her relationship with Sebastian, and Ethan knew her well enough to understand that.

"We've made peace with the past," she said, hoping he'd take her explanation for the vague one it was.

"You did more than that and you know it." Ethan paused, then said, "Parker told me that he called Sebastian one morning and he woke you both. Together."

Her cheeks burned with embarrassment. She'd never discussed her love life with Ethan, and she didn't intend to start now. "That's none of your business."

A flush rose to his face, telling her he wasn't any more comfortable with the direction of this conversation than she was.

He cleared his throat. "I never thought I'd have to say this, but it is my business if you hurt my brother."

His words came like a painful blow. "I wouldn't hurt him," she said, trying not to be offended by the insinuation. But coming from Ethan, a man she considered *her* older brother, it hurt. "How could you suggest such a thing?"

Ethan grasped both her hands in his and met her gaze. "I saw how he looked at you, Ashley. And my playboy brother, the man who's never had a relationship that meant anything to him other than fun, he's fallen for you. Hard."

She opened her mouth, then closed it again. Last night Sebastian had been trying to cajole her back into bed. He'd also alluded to the fact that they both had feelings for each other, and she'd known he was right.

"He's in love with you," Ethan said.

Her heart began to race in triple time. "No," she said, panicking at the thought. "He doesn't do love or relationships. We agreed when we started that we were both the same. We understood each other."

Ethan sighed. "Well, something's changed for him. And I suspect for you, too, but you're fighting it.

Afraid to trust because everyone in your life has always let you down."

At the stark truth and painful reminder, tears welled in her eyes and threatened to fall. "You never let me down," she whispered, holding on to the one truth that helped her through so many otherwise lonely times.

"And maybe Sebastian's grown up enough that he won't do it again."

"I live in London," she said, fighting him because she didn't know any other way but to be self-sufficient and independent ... and across the ocean from the first man who'd broken her heart.

No matter how much she felt for him now, could she really uproot her life? Not that he'd even asked her to. Surely Ethan was reading too much into a few glances between them.

"There's always a job here for you. A place here." Ethan touched his heart.

Her thoughts went immediately to how badly *he'd* been hurt. "You're such a good man. I'm sorry about everything you're going through."

He shook his head in a chiding gesture. "Changing the subject when you don't like what I'm saying. Some things stay the same," he said, nailing her behavior accurately.

She forced a smile, his words from earlier staying

with her. He'd given her a lot to think about, and her stomach was twisting badly.

But she had to focus on Ethan and what he need-ed right now, and that was a lot easier than thinking about herself. "Promise me you'll lean on your family. You won't withdraw into your penthouse and suffer in silence," she said.

"I promise you I'm dealing with all this as best I can."

It was the most she was going to get from him, and she had no choice but to accept it. As for her relationship with Sebastian, she wasn't sure what she was going to do. She had her life in London, but she couldn't deny her feelings for him, either. Something had to give, and she didn't know if she should follow her head … or her heart.

ASHLEY DIDN'T HAVE work to do, and Ethan didn't need her in the office. Although she really could have gone back to London, the sad truth was, she was in no rush to go back. Sebastian was right. She didn't want to face Jonathan and his relentless pursuit, and since she had the extra week, she intended to take it.

She didn't make muffins for Ethan, knowing he'd had enough of her hovering. She did, however, decide to enjoy her time in New York City. She started by buying tickets for a show on Wednesday and planned to go to a popular lunch restaurant on Tuesday. She left Ethan alone, knowing he was working through his pain, and no matter how much she wanted to be with Sebastian, she believed it was better not to give him the wrong idea about what she wanted from him. Not when she didn't yet know the answer to that herself.

She read a book on her phone during lunch and stopped for a manicure before heading back to the apartment. She let herself in and came to a halt. The entire kitchen counter was now filled with gorgeous roses. She didn't care how cliché, the gesture touched her heart.

She walked over to where a card sat in front of one of the vases. Pulling it out of the envelope, she read out loud. "Roses are red, violets are blue, you might live in London, but I still want you. Sebastian."

She held the card against her heart and sighed. The man had an amazing sense of humor on top of his sweetness. Knowing she couldn't avoid him after this, she took the elevator to his floor and knocked on his door.

He answered, wearing a pair of gray sweats ... and nothing else. She glanced at his bare chest and swallowed a groan.

"Can I help you?" he asked, an amused grin lifting the corners of his mouth. That sexy dimple teased her.

"I wanted to thank you for the flowers."

"You're welcome. Want to come in?" He stepped aside.

But she already stood too close to him, was aware of the smell of his cologne, the masculine scent a powerful aphrodisiac. All she really wanted to do was reach out and touch that broad chest. Run her fingers through the light sprinkling of hair. Brush her lips over his.

Instead she cleared her throat. "I really shouldn't."

He raised an eyebrow. "Afraid to be alone with me?" he asked, tongue in cheek. But he really wasn't teasing. He obviously knew that was the truth.

"Don't be ridiculous," she lied. "I just have … things to do in my apartment."

"Like what? Laundry? Washing your hair?" He chuckled, obviously aware she was making excuses so they didn't end up in bed. "Enjoy your flowers," he said, and closed the door, shutting her out.

Just as she'd suggested she wanted.

Frustrated, more with herself than with him, she headed back downstairs, took a long shower … and did, in fact, wash her hair.

Wednesday arrived and she went to a wonderful Broadway show, enjoying herself even if she had gone alone. She couldn't deny that she'd have had a better time if she'd had company. Like Sebastian. But she was sticking to her making-a-clean-break resolution.

She kept busy doing touristy things through Friday. That evening, she returned to her apartment and let herself inside. This time, a chocolate basket with a big blue Ghirardelli bow on top waited for her. She walked over and took in the items, which included a box of chocolate-covered pretzels, chocolate squares, dark chocolate with sea salt caramel, chocolate chip cookies, and of course a supply of Ghirardelli chocolate bars. She inhaled deeply, imagining that she could smell the chocolate despite the wrapping.

This time there was no card, but she knew who the gift was from and the sentiment behind it. She sat down with a sigh. What was she doing, torturing herself by staying away from Sebastian?

When a knock sounded on her door, she jumped up to answer it, hoping it was him. Instead it was Sierra.

Wearing a pair of black slacks and a light cream sweater, the other woman looked nervous as she stood in the doorway.

"Hi," Ashley said.

"Hi. I was hoping we could talk?" Sierra asked.

Surprised, Ashley stepped aside. "Come inside."

Sierra walked in and her gaze immediately went to the array of red roses and the chocolate basket Ashley had taken apart, item by item, and left on the table.

"Hungry?" Ashley asked, laughing.

"No, thank you, but wow. Sebastian's really gone all out."

Ashley blushed. "How do you know it's all from your brother?"

"Seriously? I saw how he looked at you the other day in Ethan's office. You totally grounded him and gave him the courage to tell Ethan what he needed to know."

"I didn't realize anyone else noticed," Ashley murmured.

"It was hard not to. Sebastian's never been head over heels before. It's pretty obvious."

Ashley felt a flush rise to her face. "I don't know about that." The head over heels part, she thought. "We're..." She wasn't going to tell Sierra she'd been sleeping with her brother.

"Right." Sierra put her hands to her now red cheeks, getting the message. Her pretty engagement ring sparkled from her finger.

"Congratulations, by the way," Ashley said. "On your upcoming wedding."

"Oh! Thank you. It's in a few months, and I feel like I have so much still to do."

Ashley smiled. "I can't imagine," she murmured.

"But I'll manage. My fiancé's been so helpful. But back to the reason I'm here."

Ashley waited, while Sierra stepped farther inside before turning around to face her. "You're really close with Ethan, and you're in some sort of relationship with Sebastian." Sierra drew a deep breath. "I thought we should talk."

"Okay." Ashley didn't know what to say. "Would you like to sit first?" she offered.

Sierra shook her head. "I just need to get this out. I'm sorry."

"Whatever for?" Ashley asked.

"When you came to live with us, when your mother married my father, I was a total bitch to you."

With a shake of her head, Ashley let out a laugh. "I wouldn't say you were a bitch. You just didn't..."

"Do anything to make your life easier. I wasn't warm or friendly. I didn't introduce you to my friends. I left you to sink or swim on your own, and that sucked." She swallowed hard. "I'm embarrassed now. By how jealous I was of you then. I was worried if I took you around my friends, they'd like you better than me."

Ashley was shocked. "Really? I just figured you didn't want another girl in the house."

"That, too?" Sierra shook her head and sighed. "You couldn't pay me to go back to being a teenager."

"Agreed." Ashley slid her hands into the front pockets of her jeans. "But Sierra? You don't owe me an apology. You didn't do anything awful to me. And we're adults now. It's all good. I promise."

"Thank you," she said, relief in her voice. "Because something tells me you're going to be around a lot more, and I wanted to get everything out in the open."

Ashley chose not to correct her, not wanting to get into a conversation about herself and Sebastian or her imminent return abroad. Not when she was still so confused herself.

Sierra leaned forward and pulled Ashley into a hug, taking her by surprise. "Thank you for being so great about everything." She stepped back and smiled. "You're good for my brother. I approve," she said, then turned and walked out, leaving Ashley speechless.

She shut the door behind Sierra and leaned her head against it, her heart beating hard in her chest. Because she needed to see Sebastian and be with him, talk to him, and get a handle on herself and her feelings.

Before she could lose her nerve, she headed up to his apartment and knocked on the door, a feeling of déjà vu overtaking her. Except tonight she was going to go inside.

She heard noise, then the turn of the lock, and found herself face-to-face with a pretty dark-haired woman.

"What do you want?" the woman asked, her gaze

taking in Ashley, who wore a pair of jeans and an unflattering band tee shirt, while this woman was dressed to impress.

Ashley's stomach churned at the sight of another woman in Sebastian's home.

"Dammit, Veronica, I told you I'd get it." Sebastian's voice traveled to her as he flung open the door. "Ashley," he said, obviously stunned to see her there.

She blinked hard. "What's going on?" she asked.

"Veronica was just leaving." He met Ashley's gaze without blinking.

"But Sebastian—" Veronica reached for him with her long, manicured nails.

No sooner had the woman touched him than Ashley snapped. "He said you were leaving, so just go. And get your claws off him."

Stunned, Veronica looked from Ashley to Sebastian. "It's not your apartment, so it's not your place to tell me what to do."

"But it's mine, and she's right. You need to leave," he said, shaking her off, his voice adamant.

Her expression turned angry. "Fuck you, Sebastian. You really suck. You know that?"

He shrugged. "Maybe so but I never lied to you about what I wanted."

With a huff, Veronica stormed off in her heels and a cloud of expensive perfume.

"What did she want?" Ashley asked, just as the elevator door opened and Veronica stepped inside.

He ran a hand through his already messed hair. "To see me because I hadn't been taking her calls." He answered immediately, not pausing to think up an explanation.

Ashley definitely knew who Sebastian had been before she'd returned to New York. Before he'd had the revelations he'd confided in her about and had decided to change. But was that Sebastian now?

He grasped her hand. "She doesn't mean anything to me." He blew out a shaky breath. "Look, I know I handled women badly before you, but I never led them on. I never allowed them to think there was a future when there wasn't. I told her there was no us, that she needed to leave, and the office called. I took it in the bedroom, thinking she'd go." He paused, then said, "I honestly didn't know she was still here until you knocked and she yelled out that she'd get it." He spread his hands in a gesture of honesty. He didn't look away or flinch, which told her a lot about what was or wasn't going on here.

"Do you believe me?" he asked, his voice uncertain, worried for the first time.

She nodded without hesitation. He might have been a playboy at one time, but she knew he'd had a true revelation and wanted to be a better man. She believed in him, knew he had become the person he wanted to be. Sebastian wouldn't be sending her flowers and candy, romancing her while sleeping with someone else.

He just wouldn't.

He answered her with a kiss. One that took her off guard, when she'd been so carefully keeping them apart. She'd come here to thank him for the chocolate, not to fall into his arms.

But it was so easy and it felt so right. Opening to him came naturally to her, as if he was the only one meant for her. And soon they'd made their way to the bed, tumbling onto the mattress.

Chapter Eleven

S EBASTIAN PULLED ASHLEY on top of him, feeling her body mold into his. He kissed her, lost in her taste, her warmth, and sweetness. He'd been on a campaign to win her heart, beginning with flowers and chocolates, but that was superficial, he knew. A way to keep him in her mind while giving her the space she'd asked for. But he didn't miss the fact that each time he'd left her a present, she'd come by in person to thank him.

As if she couldn't stay away.

He couldn't fucking believe Veronica had shown up here, but the fact that Ashley believed in him meant everything. She hadn't hesitated when he'd asked. Her trust told him a lot about how she felt for him now, that she knew that he wasn't the man he'd been when she showed up in town.

He slid his hands down her curves. "You feel good." His lips glided over her cheek, traced her jawbone. "I love touching you." He licked her skin. "Tasting you."

I love you, he thought, but the words lodged in the back of his throat.

He'd spent so much time showing her that they were meant to be, that he wanted her to stay here with him, without saying the words, hoping for her to come to the conclusion on her own. She was close, and he intended to make love to her until she couldn't mistake his intent.

Except, he realized, he'd taken the condoms to San Francisco, and she'd packed them in her bag. "We need to go downstairs," he said. "Condoms are in your apartment."

She groaned, opening her heavy-lidded eyes and meeting his gaze. "That's so unfair."

He chuckled, his body in full agreement with that assessment. "Let's go," he said. "I'll make it worth your while." Because he fully intended not only to make love to her but to put all his cards on the table when it came to telling her how he felt about her.

Laughing and sexually frustrated, they made their way to her place. Luckily they didn't run into anyone in the elevator who would take one look at Sebastian and know what they intended to do when they were alone.

Finally they were back at her apartment and in her bedroom. Although he'd planned to take things slow, the undressing came in a rush for them both. Then

Ashley retrieved the condoms from the bathroom and tossed them onto the bed before easing herself back against the pillows.

He took in her body, pale, silky skin, gorgeous breasts, tight nipples, and wet pussy just waiting for him, and his cock hardened even more. He grabbed his erection and pumped with his hand, groaning out loud.

"What are you waiting for?" she asked him in a husky voice. She held one hand out to him.

He knelt over her, rubbing his cock along her sex. Her eyes dilated and her hips bucked up, desire sweeping over him, pre-come on the head of his dick. Then he eased himself inside her, gliding in, drawing out the motion, letting her feel every inch as he entered her.

"Oh, Sebastian." She clasped herself around him, and he was drowning in her damp heat.

But he was determined to make this different than any time they'd been together before. He wanted to shock her into acknowledging her feelings.

"Move," she said, squeezing him tight.

He chuckled and brushed her hair off her face. "I want to savor you," he said and began to pump in and out, his gaze never leaving hers.

Never letting her break eye contact with him.

His hips rolled into hers as he drew out and slid

back in. Their bodies rocked in unison, the waves of pleasure drawing him under, swamping him with the beauty of what they shared.

"I love you, Ashley." He kissed her then, his lips soft on hers as they rocked their way to an explosive orgasm, so incredible he felt it in his chest as he gave her his heart.

She gasped at his words, just as her own orgasm hit. "Sebastian, oh my God. I love you, too," she said, riding out her climax, squeezing him tight, holding on to him, her body agreeing with the words she'd finally given him.

But he knew her well enough to understand that those words didn't mean he'd definitely keep her here. He still had work to do to convince her that her life could and should be with him. And though it wasn't a lot, he still had time.

After he disposed of the condom and slid back into bed, she cuddled into him, her soft, sated body warm against his. They didn't talk, and he didn't want to ruin the moment. Instead he was content as she drifted off, her breaths soft and even. And because he had her in his arms, he fell into a deep sleep, too.

ASHLEY WOKE UP surrounded by heat. She hadn't felt this good since she'd slept in Sebastian's bed during their trip to California. She pulled in a deep breath, inhaling his musky, masculine scent, when last night came back to her.

Along with the words they'd shared.

I love you.

Oh my God, that had been the last thing she'd expected to come from his mouth ... or to tumble out of hers. But what they'd experienced with their bodies last night had been beyond sex. Beyond anything even in her wildest dreams.

What did she do with that?

How could she give up the life she'd created during her time abroad? Yet how could she leave him behind? Anxiety and panic began to claw at her. She needed to breathe air that didn't smell like sex and Sebastian in order to really come to terms with what had happened between them, had snuck up on her and taken her off guard.

Before she could figure out how to slip out from under his arm that held her tight to him, a knock sounded on her door, or so she thought. She listened and the sound came again.

"Someone's here," she said, waking up Sebastian. "I need to get the door. Coming!" she called out loudly, not knowing if the person outside would hear. She jumped out of bed naked and looked around for her robe, finding it in her closet.

As she slid it on, she stepped back into the bedroom. Sebastian had pushed himself against the pillows and headboard. "What time is it?"

She glanced at the clock. "Eleven. We slept in."

She rushed to the door and glanced through the peephole. "Oh my God," she muttered at the sight of Jonathan standing on the other side.

She swallowed hard and tightened the sash on her short silk bathrobe. Knowing she had no choice, she opened the door and greeted him.

"Jonathan!" She couldn't keep the shock from her voice.

"Ashley, it's so wonderful to see you." He stepped toward her, clearly expected a hug or a warm greeting, but she held her ground.

"It's a surprise to see you. What are you doing in New York?"

"I decided it was enough with the distance. We needed to talk in person."

"But I told you we were over." She really was perplexed by his behavior. True, he was persistent when he wanted something, which was why he was so successful in his job, but he wasn't deaf. She'd been very clear about her feelings.

"I believe that, as soon as you spend time with me again, you'll see how perfect we are for one another. We enjoy the same restaurants and movies, yes?" He didn't wait for her to agree. "We both enjoy being home in the evenings with a nice glass of wine. We get along very well. I'm sure you thought about that while you've been away."

"Well—"

"She's been a little too busy to be thinking about anyone but me," Sebastian said, striding across the family room and joining them by the still-open door.

She swallowed hard. "Why don't we take this inside. Jonathan, come in and shut the door." She glanced at Sebastian.

He wore his jeans, button undone, feet bare, arms folded over that expansive, muscular chest. His eyes were narrowed, stare hard. Her gaze drifted to Jonathan, in his long-sleeve, V-neck sweater, looking buttoned up and stiff by comparison.

Oh God. How had she gotten herself into this situation? She'd been nothing but honest with Jonathan from the minute he'd proposed.

"Who is this?" Jonathan asked, obviously affronted and insulted by the mere fact that a man had walked out of her bedroom, half-naked.

"Sebastian Knight, this is Jonathan Davies."

Sebastian didn't extend his hand. Ever the English gentleman, Jonathan did, but Sebastian still didn't shake his hand. He remained icy.

"I'm not going to ask what's going on. It's quite

obvious," Jonathan said, anger highlighting his cheeks. "But I've come all this way, and we do need to talk." His gaze fell to Ashley.

She nodded in agreement. They did. For whatever reason, Jonathan hadn't taken her words seriously, and he needed to understand, regardless of her situation with Sebastian, she never would have married him.

Blowing out a slow breath, she turned to Sebastian. "He's right. We apparently have unfinished business." She hesitantly touched his still-folded arm. "I need to talk to him. Alone."

A muscle ticked in his jaw on his handsome face, one that only worked when he was furious. One she found endearing and always wanted to touch and smooth out, to calm him down.

Her heart felt torn in two. She didn't want to talk to Jonathan, she had to. Before she could figure her life out at all, she needed this door to be completely closed.

"Fine. I'm going to get dressed," he muttered, not at all graciously. Which didn't surprise her.

Jonathan didn't say a word while Sebastian walked into the bedroom, returning a few seconds later in his rumpled shirt and shoes.

He started to walk past her to the door, then stopped and turned.

"Sebastian?"

He grasped her forearms and pulled her toward him, sealing his lips over hers. He kissed her hard, his mouth unyielding and possessive. From behind her, she heard Jonathan gasp, but that didn't stop her body from yielding to him, and when she did, his lips softened, his tongue licking over her bottom lip before he let her go. She gave him whatever reassurance she could with her kiss, but they both knew so much between them was up in the air and uncertain.

Meeting her gaze, he mouthed the words, "I love you," before brushing past Jonathan and walking out the door, slamming it behind him.

❖   ❖   ❖

DAMMIT, DAMMIT, DAMMIT. Sebastian couldn't believe he'd fucking left her with that English prick. Yes, he understood she had unfinished business with the asshole, considering he didn't know how to take no for an answer. And by that kiss, he knew damn well she loved *him*. But what he didn't know was where Ashley would ultimately end up. Because despite her feelings, her job, her apartment, her friends, hell, her *life* was in London. And so was Mr. Nice Guy.

At one time, Sebastian would have gone to Ethan, his older brother and father figure, with his problems, but Ethan was dealing with too much of his own baggage to burden him now. So Sebastian headed to

Parker's apartment and banged on the door.

His brother opened and let him in. "You look like shit," Parker said.

Sebastian didn't crack a smile. "I feel like it, too."

"Want to talk? Or just want company?" Parker asked.

Sebastian groaned. "Both."

"Soda?"

"Yeah."

Parker headed to the kitchen and Sebastian to the family room. Parker returned with two cans of Coke, handing him one.

Sebastian popped the top and took a long, fizzy sip. "Ashley's ex-boyfriend showed up on her doorstep this morning. And I fucking left her alone with him."

Parker put his soda down on the table. "That was big of you."

With another muttered curse, Sebastian lowered himself into a chair, took a drink, and put the can down. "I'm not sure I had a choice. She says she's told him it's over in no uncertain terms, but here he is because he couldn't take no for an answer. She wanted time to talk to him, and I gave it to her."

Parker nodded, eyeing him with concern. "I've never seen you torn up over a woman."

"It's Ashley. It's always been Ashley. Since I was

eighteen and fucked up by letting Dad send her away. She's the only woman who's ever understood me. She sees me," he said. "She gets me. She makes me whole."

A shit-eating grin lifted his brother's lips as he flopped onto the sofa. "Though I never thought I'd see the day, I can't deny she's good for you."

"But she's not mine. Not the way I want or need. She's made it clear her life is in London, and with the prick begging her to stay, who knows what she'll do."

"Did you ask her to stay?"

He shook his head, his chest squeezing tight. "I was trying to play the long game. She's been panicked since we got back from California. So I've been trying to win her over. Last night I told her I loved her. *Stay with me* would have been next."

But he realized now that the long game might have been his mistake and downfall, because she didn't know for certain he wanted her here, in New York.

Parker let him talk, think, reason through his feelings, something his middle brother had always been good at. Ethan gave directions. Parker listened and let you come to your own conclusions.

So Sebastian continued to reason with himself. Yeah, he'd told her he'd changed, and he'd proven it with actions, but he hadn't said he wanted a future. "Fuck!"

"Want to go down there and interrupt? Stake your claim?"

He shook his head. Restraint came at a heavy price, but he knew damn well storming in again would be a mistake. "Ashley would kill me. She needs to figure things out for herself."

And that meant giving her the time she needed with her ex from London.

No matter how much it was eating Sebastian alive.

He rose to his feet. "I'm going to shower and go to the office for a while. I need to keep busy or I'm going to go insane."

Parker stood. He walked over and put a hand on his shoulder. "I've seen how she looks at you. Hold on to hope," he said.

"Thanks."

Sebastian headed to his apartment, deep in thought. He didn't miss the irony of his current situation. For so long, everything in life had come easy for him, especially women. A wink, a smile, a few charming words, and they fell into his bed. Now, the one time he desperately wanted something for keeps, he couldn't just reach out and take it. The ball was in her court, and he had no choice but to wait.

ASHLEY WATCHED SEBASTIAN leave, her heart in her

throat, waiting for the slam of the door before turning to face her ex. And that's what he was, her *ex*-boyfriend, no matter how persistent or obstinate he chose to be.

"Jonathan," she said, speaking slowly and carefully. "I realize this is awkward, but—"

"Awkward? You've been with another man!"

"But not cheating on you. I ended things. I never wanted to hurt you, but I was perfectly clear that we weren't going to get engaged, that I didn't love you the way I needed to in order to say yes."

A muscle throbbed in his temple. She didn't find it attractive the way she did when Sebastian clenched his jaw and the tiny muscle there ticked and gave away his anger and frustration.

"I seriously thought if we could just see each other again…"

She shook her head. "I'm sorry but it isn't happening."

"But you're coming back to London, yes?"

Her stomach cramped hard at the question.

Without waiting for an answer, he said, "Maybe we could pick up where we left off before I proposed. Take it slower. You could grow to care for me that way. I've thought about it and we could be so good together."

"Oh, Jonathan. No. Even if I come back to London, we're over."

"I see…" His voice trailed off as reality set in. "Well, this is quite embarrassing."

"I'm sorry you made the trip for nothing." She didn't want to rub in the fact that she'd been clear all along.

"Wait. What do you mean, if you come back to London?" He picked up on her choice of words earlier. "Your life is there. Your job. Friends. Your apartment. How could you just leave it all behind and not come home?" he asked, truly stunned at the notion. "Is it about him? Sebastian?"

She rubbed her hands over her burning eyes. "I have a life there, yes," she said, thinking through her words as she spoke them out loud.

But something Jonathan just said kept circling in her brain. *How could you just leave it all behind and not come home?* he'd asked.

Where was home?

Was it the apartment she'd locked up and walked away from in London that felt colder and emptier in her mind than the one she was standing in now?

Was it the job there that she liked but could do anywhere? *There's always a job here for you. A place here,* Ethan had said. Ethan, the only family she'd ever had. He was in New York. He wanted her here.

Was it the friends she'd made in England, but who

212

she didn't feel particularly close to? Because she'd never been a girl to make a BFF. Yet when Sierra had walked away after their talk, Ashley had had the distinct feeling that she could be close with her now if she gave the other woman a chance.

Or was home Sebastian? The man who filled the empty pieces inside her. The man who made her smile when she was sad, who understood her past, who she'd always been able to talk to and confide in, from the time she'd been sixteen years old? A man who made love to her so tenderly he held her heart in his hands?

"Ashley? Where in the world did you go?" Jonathan asked loudly, bringing her back to the present. "I said your name quite a few times." He looked at her, concern on his face.

A face she found good-looking, but not pulse-pounding, life-alteringly handsome. He didn't make her question everything she'd ever believed about sex and love. Sebastian did.

"I'm sorry, Jonathan. I won't be coming back to London because it isn't home. It was a place to live, to stay when I thought I didn't have anything for me here. But I was wrong."

"This is about Sebastian." He sounded defeated.

"In part, yes," she admitted. "But it's also about me. And during my time here, I've come to realize that

I stayed away from these people too long. I didn't give them a chance to be my family. And they are."

Shoulders slumped now, he nodded. "I really do hear you now," he said. "I understand and I wish you well."

"I wish you the same," she said. "And I hope one day you find a woman who will make you question everything you ever believed was true about life."

He looked at her quizzically, confused. She really did hope he figured it out one day, she thought, as she walked him to the door and said goodbye.

Because thanks to Sebastian, she understood so much more now. It had been easy to tell herself she didn't want a forever relationship, that she didn't believe in love before she'd experienced those emotions.

Now she couldn't imagine living without them.

She couldn't imagine being without Sebastian.

SEBASTIAN SPENT A few hours at the office, which was quiet on a Saturday. Nobody was in and he had the place to himself. After going over some paperwork and killing as much time as he could manage, he decided to go home. Throughout the day, he hadn't heard from Ashley on his phone, and the thought made his stomach churn.

He didn't know what to expect when he saw her next, but he knew he needed an answer to one very important question. Was she staying in New York or returning to London? Up until now, she'd been adamant about going back.

But last night she'd told him she loved him. Either that changed things for her or it didn't. But he couldn't go on living with that uncertainty hanging over his head.

He promised himself that if she told him she was leaving, he'd let her go like a man, without begging her to stay. Because one thing he knew for sure, she had to be the one to come to him on her own. No pressure.

He wouldn't be like her ex, begging for scraps.

He'd handle rejection like a man.

✧   ✧   ✧

WHEN ASHLEY WENT to Sebastian's apartment and found he wasn't there, she was disappointed. And nervous. Where had he gone after she'd sent him away so she could be with Jonathan?

She didn't know what was going on in Sebastian's mind, but she wasn't going down without a fight. She went to Ethan's and talked him into letting her into Sebastian's apartment so she could wait for him.

When time began to pass and the afternoon headed toward evening, she decided she'd make him dinner so they could talk when he returned. But since she hadn't thought things out, and going through his cabinets she didn't find much, she had nothing to cook for him but spaghetti and jarred sauce. It would have to do.

She found wine he'd obviously gotten from Sei Bellisimo and poured herself a glass of red, reliving the moments they'd spent together at the vineyard. She realized she was making herself at home in his apartment without being invited. At that thought, she took another long sip and stirred the sauce in the pan.

She had music playing from her phone, soft love songs, to torture herself with as she waited. Finally, she heard the sound of the key in the lock, and her heart began racing in her chest as Sebastian let himself inside.

She shut the stove top off and rubbed her hands on her jeans, blowing out a deep breath.

"Who's here?" he called out, just as she met him in the entryway.

"Hi." She treated him to an awkward wave.

"Ashley." His voice sounded wary, his expression emotionless. "What are you doing here?"

She rubbed her hands on the front of her jeans, on her thighs. "Ethan let me in to wait. You were gone a long time, so I decided to make myself busy and I started dinner. You didn't have much to work with," she said, realizing she was so nervous she was rambling.

He tossed his keys on the credenza. "Where's lover boy?"

"He left. I assume he's on his way back to London."

Sebastian raised an eyebrow. "He get the message this time?"

"For certain." She shoved her hands into her front pockets, feeling awkward because he wasn't making this easy.

His guard was up, and for that she didn't blame him.

"Sebastian, I'm sorry about Jonathan. About asking you to leave, but I had to close that door once and for all."

Without answering, he walked into his family room, and she followed, letting him process her words. Finally, he turned to her, and in his eyes, she saw the pain she'd caused him, in his face, the anxiety he felt thanks to her.

"It's not the ex that has me worked up," he said.

She came up to him and put her hand on his shoulder. "Then what is it?"

What could she do to get the soft, tender Sebastian back? The one without walls between them.

"It's you. It's all the uncertainty between us."

She knew then what she had to do. "I love you, that's certain." Her hand slid upward, stroking his cheek. "And I realize we both came into this with no expectations. We both agreed we didn't do relationships. Personally, I didn't even believe in love, but you taught me that it really does exist."

He grasped her wrist. "It's not enough. You've also said, over and over, that your life is in London. If you expect me to have any kind of long-distance relationship, you need to know that's off the table. It's all or nothing, Ashley. And I want all of you, right here, in New York. With me."

She blew out a relieved breath. If there was any part of her that worried that, though he loved her, he didn't want a future, that part was now put to rest.

"I know I'm asking a lot," he went on, unaware of her feelings. His grip on her wrist tightened with his words. Nerves. She felt his nerves as well as her own. "And I know your life is there. Your home is there, and I'm asking you to give up everything to be with me. It's selfish. But that's what I'm asking for."

She smiled so wide it hurt. "That's really good to know, because while I was making dinner, I was wondering if me, here, is something you'd like to come home to every night."

"Wait. What?" He froze, as if afraid he hadn't heard her correctly.

She met his gaze, willing him to understand. "You're wrong when you say London is my home. *You're* my home, Sebastian. You make me feel things I never believed were possible. Your love is worth giving up London for, because staying here, I get everything."

He picked her up, surprising her, and she squealed as he spun her around, placing her down on her feet so he could kiss her, long and hard.

"You're my everything," he said, his smile as big as hers. "You understand me. You believe in me. You make me whole, giving me something I never understood I needed. And if I could give up my whole life for you, I would. Instead I promise you will never regret staying here."

"Why would I? You're here. My family is here. My *life* is here."

Suddenly, he dropped to his knees and she gasped. "This is spontaneous, unplanned, and will be a great story to tell our children, but Ashley, I want you to marry me. To be my partner. My better half. My everything." He reached for her hand and she placed it inside of his. "Ring to follow," he said with a charming grin. "So what do you say?"

"I say yes."

Upon hearing that, he rose to his feet, picked her up, and carried her into the bedroom, where he stripped off first her clothes, then his, and proceeded to seal their agreement in the way they did best.

He made love to her.

He made her his.

Epilogue

SEBASTIAN ACCOMPANIED ASHLEY to London to sever her lease, pack up her apartment, quit her job, and say her goodbyes. It wasn't that he thought she'd see the place she'd lived for so long and change her mind about him and moving to New York permanently, but he was hedging his bets by accompanying her every step of the way.

Before they left, he took her to Tiffany, where he insisted she pick out her engagement ring. Considering she was going to be wearing it *for the rest of her life*, he wanted her to love everything about the special piece of jewelry.

Due for a new iPhone, he went into the Apple store to purchase one, whereupon he deleted every number that was formerly his black book of women. He'd never be needing those digits again. He couldn't believe he'd ever been that man. He was so much happier now, knowing he could look in the mirror and both like and respect the guy staring back.

Unfortunately, Ethan had fallen into a funk after

the California revelations, but the news that Ashley was moving home had helped his mood. Knowing she'd be a real part of the family also soothed the beast in him somewhat. The man did like having his family together.

Parker was Parker, thrilled they were engaged, but still antsy and hard to read. Ever since he'd had to give up the sport he loved and settle into a desk job, Sebastian had worried about him. Ethan did, too. But until he made peace with his life, there was little anyone could do for him.

Sebastian was now all about romance, and he was convinced that a good woman would solve all Parker's problems. His middle brother didn't want to hear it. Soon, he'd be taking a trip to scope out places for a Knight Time Technology corporate retreat. Hopefully getting out of the office and spending time away would be good for his soul.

With Sierra getting married soon, a huge church affair with a country club afterward, Sebastian and Ashley had agreed to a small, intimate family gathering next month. Not only did Ashley not want to steal the spotlight from Sierra, she didn't want the big trappings of a large event.

She just wanted his ring on her finger and their lives intertwined. He couldn't agree more. He'd give her anything she asked for. Even if it meant having their parents in the same room for the first time in what felt like forever, they'd survive. There was always a chance one of them would be too busy to show up… Both Sebastian and Ashley would be fine with that.

As long as they were together.

Next up in The Knight Brothers Series is TAKE ME TONIGHT, Parker's story:

TAKE ME TONIGHT

He was going through the motions… and then he met her.

Parker Knight had and lost it all. Now he works for his family's business, wearing a suit and pretending to be happy. A weekend away to plan a corporate retreat turns into a revelation when he lays eyes on Emily Stevens, the sexy owner of a small lodge that's seen better days. One look at Emily and the run down resort and suddenly Parker has a purpose. He turns his short stay into a longer one, intending to act on the intense chemistry and desire that runs hot between them. While there, he plans to save Emily and her aging father's business with an infusion of cash and manpower.

But Emily doesn't trust slick city guys, especially one who is going to leave when his time off is over. No matter how incredible he makes her feel, in bed and out.

Parker has his hands full, not only with a wary Emily but with someone who doesn't want the lodge to succeed, and if things keep getting worse, not even a Knight can save her.

Want even more Carly books?
CARLY'S BOOKLIST by Series – visit:
http://smarturl.it/CarlyBooklist

Sign up for Carly's Newsletter:
http://smarturl.it/carlynews

Carly on Facebook:
facebook.com/CarlyPhillipsFanPage

Carly on Instagram:
instagram.com/carlyphillips

About the Author

Carly Phillips is the *N.Y. Times* and *USA Today* Best-selling Author of over 50 sexy contemporary romance novels featuring hot men, strong women and the emotionally compelling stories her readers have come to expect and love. Carly's career spans over a decade and a half with various New York publishing houses, and she is now an Indie author who runs her own business and loves every exciting minute of her publishing journey. Carly is happily married to her college sweetheart, the mother of two nearly adult daughters and three crazy dogs (two wheaten terriers and one mutant Havanese) who star on her Facebook Fan Page and website. Carly loves social media and is always around to interact with her readers. You can find out more about Carly at www.carlyphillips.com.

CPSIA information can be obtained
at www.ICGtesting.com
Printed in the USA
LVHW031049120519
617539LV00014B/633/P

9 781947 089075